Victoria Torres

Unfortunately
Average

Victoria Torres, Unfortunately Average
is published by Stone Arch Books,
A Capstone Imprint
1710 Roe Crest Drive
North Mankato, Minnesota 56003
www.capstoneyoungreaders.com

Library of Congress Cataloging-in-Publication Data
Bowe, Julie, 1962– author.
 Pompom problems / by Julie Bowe.
  pages cm. —— (Victoria Torres, unfortunately average)
 Summary: Victoria Torres is new to middle school, and she decides that being a
cheerleader is the key to popularity--but the competition is stiff, especially since it
includes the awful, bossy, Annelise, and even with the support of her best friend, Bea,
Victoria needs to work on both her cartwheels and her confidence.
 ISBN 978-1-4965-0532-3 (library binding)
 ISBN 978-1-4965-0536-1 (paperback)
 ISBN 978-1-4965-2357-0 (eBook pdf)
 1. Cheerleading——Juvenile fiction. 2. Self-confidence——Juvenile fiction. 3. Self-esteem——
Juvenile fiction. 4. Best friends——Juvenile fiction. 5. Middle schools——Juvenile fiction.
[1. Cheerleading——Fiction. 2. Self-confidence——Fiction. 3. Self-esteem——Fiction. 4. Best
friends——Fiction. 5. Friendship——Fiction. 6. Middle schools——Fiction. 7. Schools——
Fiction.] I. Title.
 PZ7.B671943Po 2016
 813.6——dc23
 [Fic]   2015000108

Designer: Veronica Scott
Image credits: Capstone Studio; Newscom: Sebastian Marmaduke Image Source,
 (chihuahua) cover
Design elements: Shutterstock

Special thanks to the team of tweens who provided helpful feedback
on covers and design.

Printed in the United States of America in Stevens Point, Wisconsin.
032015   008824WZF15

POMPOM
PROBLEMS

by Julie Bowe

STONE ARCH BOOKS
a capstone imprint

All About Me

Hi, I'm Victoria Torres — Vicka for short. Not that I am short. Or tall. I'm right in the middle, otherwise known as "average height for my age." I'm almost twelve years old and just started sixth grade at Middleton Middle School. My older sister, Sofia, is an eighth grader. My little brother, Lucas, is in kindergarten, so that puts me in the middle of my family too:

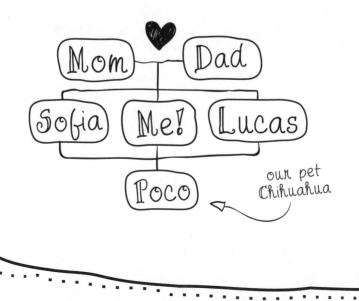

Mom ♥ Dad

Sofia   Me!   Lucas

Poco   our pet Chihuahua

I'm average in other ways too. I live in a middle-sized house at the center of an average town. I get Bs for grades, sit in the middle of the flute section in band, and can hit a baseball only as far as the shortstop. And even though she would say I'm "above average," I'm not always the BEST best friend to my BFF, Bea.

Still, my parents did name me Victoria — as in victory? They had high hopes for me right from the start! This year, I am determined to be better than average in every way!

 Me!

Chapter 1

Thwunk!

My best friend, Bea, and I see the glittery blue and gold flier stuck to our locker as soon as we get to school on Monday morning.

Hey, Muskrats!
Here's Your Chance to Shine!

Be a Middleton Middle School
Football Cheerleader!

Practices: After school
Tryouts: Next Week

Sign up in the Caf during lunch today!

"What's a Caf?" Bea asks, reading the flier. We've been sixth graders for only a few days, so we are still learning how to speak middle school.

"I think *Caf* is short for *Cafeteria*," I tell Bea.

Bea nods, thoughtfully. "Caf . . . cafeteria. Got it." She resnaps her sparkly barrettes in her dark, curly hair. "Not that it matters where the sign-up table is. The last thing we want to do is try out for cheerleading, right?"

"Wrong," I reply, tapping the bright flier with the tip of my pink-polished pointer finger. "It says here that cheerleading will make us *shine!*"

Bea blinks. "I already shine." She taps her sparkly barrettes. "Besides, we can barely do star jumps, Vicka, even though they're basically just jumping jacks. Not to mention cartwheels. And don't even get me started on the *splits!* Cheerleaders have to do stuff like that all the time. I should know. Jazmin has been cheerleading since she was our age."

Jazmin is Bea's older sister. She's in eighth grade,

just like my brainy sister, Sofia. *Unlike* Sofia, Jazmin is a cheerleader. Everything about her shines, including her braces! She even went to cheerleading camp this summer.

"But we'll be *poppies* if we make the cheerleading squad," I reply.

Bea makes a face. "*Poppies*? Is that another middle school vocab word I need to learn?"

"*Poppies* is short for *popular* girls," I explain. "I just made it up. You know, like Annelise? Don't you want to be as popular as her?" Annelise has been the most popular girl in our class since kindergarten. She and her little brother always get the newest and coolest gadgets and toys. They have big, fancy parties too, because their parents are rich. For her ninth birthday party, Annelise's parents hired a magician. For her tenth, they rented a giant bouncy castle. Last year, for her eleventh, a limo picked us up and drove us to a teen concert in the city. We even got to meet the band backstage! Who knows what they'll do this year. Fly us all to London for lunch with the queen? Sometimes I wish my parents would spoil me like that.

"Annelise is a bully, not a poppy," Bea says. "Girls only hang out with her to stay on her good side."

I sigh. What Bea said is true. Annelise bullies everyone, even her so-called friends. I don't want to be a bully. But I *do* want to be a poppy!

"But Bea," I reply, "popular girls really know how to shine. That's why they always wear cool sunglasses. To shield their eyes from the glare."

Bea makes another face.

I close my eyes, imagining myself standing under the field lights, cheering in front of the packed bleachers at a Middleton Muskrats football game! My family is there. Dad is wearing his lucky baseball cap and whistling through his fingers. Mom is waving the glittery Muskrat pendant she made from her scrapbooking supplies. Lucas is jumping around and waving the pendant he made out of duct tape and toilet paper tubes. And Sofia, hunched a few seats away, is adjusting her earbuds and pretending she doesn't know them. All while I shake two shiny blue and gold pompoms and yell my lungs out.

Kids from my class are there too — even some of the boys like Henry, Sam, and Drew. *Especially* Drew. I've had a crush on him since this summer when he did a cannonball off the side of the Middleton Municipal Pool and totally drenched me with water. He cracked up when he saw me standing there, dripping. Then he splashed even more water at me!

At first, I was angry because I hadn't changed into my swimsuit yet. But then he bought a blue ice pop at the concessions stand and shared it with me to say he was sorry. Blue is my favorite flavor! Everyone knows that boys are ice pop hogs. They only share them if they like you.

Does Drew like me? I'm not sure, but I do like him. No one knows this, except for Bea.

When I open my eyes again, Bea is still making

the face. "I don't care about being a poppy. All I care about is getting to class on time. C'mon, or we'll be late!"

"Pleeeease, Bea," I beg, as she drags me down the hallway. "I want to be a cheerleader more than anything, and I *need* to be a poppy. Try out for the squad with me!"

Bea stops and rolls her pretty eyes, which are even browner than mine. "Fine," she says. "I'll sign up with you, but not because I want to be a cheerleader or need to be popular. I'll try out because you're my BFF."

I give Bea a hug. "You won't regret it, Bea! Our world is about to change!"

I step back and do an awkward star jump. Fortunately, Bea ducks before I whack the barrettes out of her hair. *Un*fortunately, my hand smacks against a locker.

Thwunk!

"¡Ay!"

"Ouchies, Vicka!" Bea cries. "Are you okay?"

I nod, shaking away the pain in my wrist, then pushing my glasses back up on my nose. "I'm *better* than okay," I reply. "I am Victoria Torres . . . Cheerleader!"

Chapter 2

Four Simple Rules

Annelise, Katie, and Grace are waiting in line by the cheerleading table when Bea and I get to the Caf during lunch hour. It doesn't surprise me that Katie and Grace are signing up with Annelise. They stick to her like glue.

I like Katie and Grace, but Annelise and I have been enemies since last year. That's when I won the Middleton Elementary School Spelling Bee Trophy — the only trophy I've ever won in my *unfortunately average* life. It was shiny and glittery with a golden bumblebee attached to the top. But when I let Annelise hold it, she accidentally-on-purpose dropped it because she was jealous of me for beating her by one word — *Chihuahua*. When you own a pet Chihuahua, you know how to spell it!

The golden bee broke off the trophy. I tried to glue it back on, but it wouldn't stay. My little brother, Lucas, wrapped tape around it to hold the bee in place. But he used half a roll! Now it looks like I won a trophy for Best Mummy. *Grrrr.*

"Hi, Katie and Grace," I say, getting in line behind them.

"Hi, Vicka! Hi, Bea!" they reply.

Annelise turns around. She crosses her arms and narrows her icy blue eyes. "The lunch line is over there, Vicka," she says. She nudges her wickedly pointed chin in the direction of the food trays. "*This* is the line for cheerleading tryouts." Annelise cocks her head at me, making her long ponytail swing back and forth like a clock pendulum. *Tick . . . tock . . . get . . . lost.*

I link elbows with Bea. "We know this is the line for tryouts," I say. "We want to be cheerleaders!"

"Correction," Bea says. "*Vicka* wants to be a cheerleader. I'm just here to help make her dream come true."

"*You* want to be a cheerleader?" Annelise says to me, laughing. "That sounds like a nightmare, not a dream!"

Grace and Katie snicker. Annelise gives them an approving smile.

Annelise may be a bully, but she doesn't intimidate me . . . much.

I let go of Bea's arm and square my shoulders. "Cheerleaders have to yell loud. I can do that. After all, I do have a brother *and* a sister. Plus, I am very good at star jumps."

I step out of line and do a star jump to demonstrate. This time, I don't whack anything and my glasses stay in place!

Annelise sniffs. "Even my dorky little brother can do star jumps," she says. She shoves Grace and Katie out of the way. "Can you do *this*?"

Annelise raises her hands above her head and pushes off on the heel of her sparkly purple flats. Then she does a *perfect* cartwheel that ends with the *splits*, right there on the barbecue-scented lunchroom floor!

I gulp. *My* cartwheels look more like flat tires. And the only splits I've had any luck with are the kind made with ice cream and bananas.

Grace and Katie quickly applaud when Annelise looks at them. Then she stands up, smiling smugly at me. "You won't beat me *this* time, Victoria Torres."

The line moves forward.

Annelise, Katie, and Grace step up to the cheerleading table. Three older cheerleaders are sitting behind it, including Jazmin.

"Hi!" Jazmin says to all of us. "Do you girls want to be Middleton Muskrat cheerleaders?"

"Yes!" Annelise, Katie, Grace, and I shout enthusiastically.

"Not especially," Bea mumbles. "But I *do* like

pompoms." She eyes the pair of glittery blue and gold pompoms lying on the table.

"Great!" Jazmin says. "We have just four simple rules in cheerleading." She points to a sign on the table.

Middleton Middle School

Cheerleading Rules:

1. Be a positive role model.
2. Maintain good grades.
3. Attend all practices.
4. Cheer the Muskrats on to victory!

I get lots of practice being a positive role model because Mom and Dad make me be one for my little brother, Lucas. I don't get *great* grades, like my sister, Sofia, but I do get *good* grades, mostly Bs. Attending practices won't be a problem because Bea and I can walk home together afterward — we live only a few blocks from the school. And I *know* I can cheer the team onto victory — my name *is* Victoria, after all!

I reach for a pencil that's next to the sign-up sheet. Before I can pick it up, Annelise snatches it away and signs her name on the sheet. Then she gives the pencil to Katie and Grace.

As they sign their names, I look at the list. Lots of girls have already signed up for tryouts. I look at Jazmin. "How many cheerleaders do you need on the squad?"

"There are only *four* open spots," Jazmin replies.

I make buggy Chihuahua eyes. "But there are at least fourteen names on the sign-up sheet!"

"Fifteen," Bea says, taking the pencil from Grace

and writing her name. She holds the pencil out to me. "Your turn, Number 16."

"We'll practice after school, starting tomorrow," Jazmin tells us. "Meet by the football field."

Even though I'm feeling below-average about my chances of winning a spot on the squad, I take the pencil from Bea. "Go, Muskrats!" I say enthusiastically, signing my name in big bold letters.

"That's the spirit!" Jazmin says cheerfully. "You've got what it takes to be a cheerleader, Vicka!"

I look up, surprised. "Really?"

Jazmin nods. "School spirit is the number-one requirement for a Middleton Middle School cheerleader!"

I smile, feeling school spirit bubbling up inside me like a freshly shaken can of soda. I'm so excited, I do another star jump!

Thwack!

"Ouchies!"

"*¡Uf!* Sorry Bea!" I exclaim.

Annelise barks a laugh, as I give Bea a quick hug to make up for the fact that I just bonked her on the chin. "Come on, girls," Annelise says to Grace and Katie. "Let's get out of the danger zone before Vicka breaks our jaws!" They march off, giggling.

I look at Bea with concern. "Does it hurt?" I ask.

"Only when I speak," Bea says, rubbing her chin. "Can we eat now? There's mac and cheese. I can swallow that without chewing."

"Yes," I reply, glancing back over my shoulder at the blue and gold pompoms, glittering under the florescent lunchroom lights, as I walk Bea toward the food line. "But eat fast."

"Why?" Bea asks. "Our next class doesn't start for thirty minutes."

"Exactly," I reply. "We'll have time to practice cartwheels. Then, we'll move on to doing the splits. I bet a lot of girls are good at doing them, just like Annelise. We have to be the best at tryouts!"

"It's not all about cartwheels and splits, you know,"

Bea says as we get in line for our food. "You saw the cheerleading rules: school spirit, getting good grades, and showing up for games are the most important things."

I grab a food tray. "I'm not taking any chances," I say. "I have to learn how to do a *perfect* cartwheel if I want to beat Annelise. Eat fast!"

Chapter 3

Go, Muskrats, Go!

We are huffing and puffing like big, bad muskrats by the time the bell rings for afternoon classes. Between the two of us, Bea and I cartwheeled to the moon and back, which is hard work and a lot of upside-down time.

Fortunately, a water fountain is near our history classroom. We head for it dizzily down the hallway. *Un*fortunately, when we turn the corner, we run right into Annelise. The phone she's texting on flies from her hands. It *jumps, bumps, and thumps!* across the shiny tile floor.

"Watch where you're going!" Annelise shouts at us.

"Sorry," I say, chasing after the phone and giving it back to Annelise. "It was an accident. We didn't see you."

"You better not have broken it!" Annelise grumbles, tapping the screen on her phone. It blinks to life. *Whew!*

"You're not supposed to be texting between classes, anyway," Bea says to Annelise. "It's against school rules."

"Duh, Bea," Annelise replies. "It's *before* class, not between." She tucks her phone into her hoodie pocket. Then she studies us. "Why do you look so hot and sweaty? Phys ed isn't until seventh hour."

I shrug, not wanting to tell Annelise the truth. If she knows we've been practicing cartwheels, she might decide to practice too. That will put me further behind at tryouts.

"Um . . ." I say, casually, "we've just been hanging around."

"Yeah," Bea chimes in, picking bits of leaves from

her hair. She toppled to the ground a few times while we were practicing. "Just hanging around."

Annelise crosses her arms and frowns. "Hanging around? Where . . . from tree branches?"

Fortunately, the final warning bell rings. I grab Bea's arm. "Gotta go!" We start to scoot around Annelise before she can ask any more questions.

*Un*fortunately, Annelise sticks out her big foot. I trip over it, taking Bea down with me. My glasses fly. Our history books *jump, bump, and thump!* to the floor.

"I'm *so* sorry!" Annelise says, with fake concern. "It was an *accident.*" She steps on my history book as she heads into our classroom.

"Accident my *foot*," Bea grumbles. "She did that on purpose!"

"Don't get upset," I tell Bea as I put on my glasses again. "We have to set a *positive attitude.* Now hurry, or we really will be late for class!"

We gather up our books, dash down the hall, and

bolt into our classroom. "Tardy," Mrs. Larson, our history teacher, tells us.

Bea and I slump.

Annelise grins.

❀ ❀ ❀

Cheerleading practice doesn't start until tomorrow, but I don't want to let any of my school spirit wear off before then. As soon as I get home from school, I do my homework, and then I help Mom get supper ready. After supper, Lucas and Sofia help Dad with the dishes. I get busy practicing my star jumps in front of the mirror in our living room. Our house isn't big enough for cartwheels, and it's already getting dark outside.

"Go!" I shout as I raise my arms above my head and scissors kick my legs. "Muskrats!" I shout louder as I lower my arms to my sides and bring my legs together.

Poco drops his chew toy and sits up, watching me.

I do more jumping jacks, shouting louder each time.

"GO!"

"MUSKRATS!!"

"GO!!!"

Poco jumps to his tiny feet, growling like the world's smallest grizzly bear. *"Yipyipyip!"* he barks, nipping at my sneakers. Obviously, Poco is not a Muskrat fan.

"Vicka!" Mom says over the top of the newspaper she's reading. "Please do your jumping and shouting *outside*. And take Poco with you."

Poco whimpers, tucking his tail between his legs.

"But the sun is going down," I say, looking out our living room window. "And there are no mirrors in our yard. I need to make sure my stars are very *jumpy!*"

Mom sighs and moves to the couch.

I begin again.

"GO!"

"Yip!"

"MUSKRATS!!"

"*Yip!!*"

"GO . . . MUSKRATS . . . GO!!!"

"*Yipyipyip!!!*"

Mom lets the newspaper fall to her lap and closes her eyes.

Lucas darts in from the kitchen. "We've got rats?!" he asks, holding a spatula over his head like a caveman club. "Where?"

"*Musk*rats," I explain. "I'm practicing to be a cheerleader."

Lucas lets the spatula fall to his side. "*Rats*," he says. "I was hoping for a new pet."

"*No* more pets," Mom says, shooting a look at Poco. "And that's enough cheerleading for tonight, Vicka."

"But, *Mom!*" I whine. "If I don't practice, I won't be the number one Muskrat at cheerleading tryouts!"

Lucas tosses aside his spatula and starts squeaking. "*Squeak, squeak, squeak!*"

I'm not sure if he's pretending to be a rat or a

muskrat, but either way, Poco springs into guard dog mode. He chases after my ratty brother, nipping at his invisible tail as Lucas scampers around the room.

I can't stop myself. I crouch beside the couch like an alley cat and pounce when Lucas comes back around.

"*Meee-ow!*"

"*Squeeeak!*"

"*Yipyipyip!*"

Dad rushes into the room, wiping his hand on a dishtowel, soap suds clinging to his big, hairy wrists. "What's going on in here?" he shouts. "A barnyard dance?"

"Cheerleading practice!" Mom shouts back.

Lucas hops over Mom's feet. So do I. She swats at us playfully with her newspaper. "*No* rats!" she cries. "No *cats!*"

Lucas and I scream with laughter. Dad chuckles. Sofia appears behind him, potholders clamped over her ears. "Make them stop!" she hollers.

But Dad just waves his red-checkered dish towel like a bullfighter's cape as Lucas and I circle around. "Too late," he says. "The place has gone wild!"

Sofia groans. "I can't *believe* I have to live with a bunch of goofballs!"

Lucas runs up to Sofia and tags her arm. "*Squeak, squeak!* You're it, *goofball*!"

Sofia groans again. But she chases after our brother.

I collapse onto the couch, next to Mom. "Go . . . Muskrats . . . go . . ." I say, catching my breath. "Cheerleading is a lot of work!"

Sofia stops and stares at me. "Don't tell me you're trying out for the cheerleading squad?"

"*Si*," I say. "I am."

Sofia groans *again*. She's very good at groaning. "Why would you want to jump around shaking pom-poms in front of a crowd?"

"Because it will make me popular," I reply.

Sofia laughs. "All it will make you is tired, Vicka.

You have to jump, clap, and shout for the entire football game!"

"And don't forget the pompoms," Lucas adds, squeezing in between Mom and me. "You have to shake them too!"

Poco barks in agreement. He lies down at my feet, panting.

"Vicka can do anything she sets her mind to," Dad says as he corrals Sofia back to the kitchen.

"She certainly can," Mom says. Then she opens her newspaper again and starts reading the comics to Lucas.

I sink into the couch, thinking.

Jump, clap, shout, and shake pompoms all at the same time? ¡Uf!

When it comes to doing everything at once, I am below average!

Chapter 4

A Not-So-Perfect Cartwheel

The next morning, I'm in much better spirits. Bea messaged me last night with a link to a cheerleading video she found online. It was called "How to Do a Perfect Cartwheel!" We both watched it a million times.

While walking to school, we watch it once more on Bea's phone. You can tell the girl in the video has a lot of school spirit. Her voice is *loud*. Her ponytail is *bouncy*. Her cartwheel is *springy*.

"And that's how you do a perfect cartwheel!" says the loud, bouncy, springy girl at the end.

Bea taps off the screen. "I'm not nearly as springy as that girl," she says.

"Me neither," I add. Then I think for a moment. "Maybe it would help if we wore our hair in ponytails?"

Bea brightens. "Good idea!" She pulls two stretchy bands off her wrist. They even sparkle!

We clump our hair into the bounciest ponytails we can manage without combs or hairspray. I tuck my glasses into my backpack.

Then we race to the giant muskrat statue that stands outside our school, drop our backpacks, and start practicing cartwheels. Over and over, we wheel our carts, round and round the giant muskrat. "Keep your arms *straight*," I coach Bea. "Don't bend your knees. *Fling* your legs!"

A minute later, Bea steadies herself against the muskrat's giant fiberglass foot. "I'm all flung out," she says dizzily. Her face looks a little green. "I'll coach you for a while."

Bea watches as I do another cartwheel.

"How was that?" I ask. "Were my legs stick-straight?"

Bea bites her lip. "More like bendy straws."

I sigh. "I'll never be ready in time for tryouts next week. There go my poppy dreams. Poof!"

"All it takes is confidence!" Bea says.

"Okay," I reply. "I'm *confident* I will fail."

Bea sighs. "You just need to think like a cheerleader," she says. "Here, maybe this will help."

Bea runs over to her backpack, unzips it, and pulls out a blue and yellow sweatshirt.

Taking the sweatshirt from Bea, I gawk at the large *M* and fierce-looking muskrat that decorate the front of it. "This is an *official* Middleton Muskrat cheerleading hoodie!" I exclaim. "Where did you get it?"

"I 'borrowed' it from Jazmin," Bea replies. "It's her favorite one, so *don't* tell her I took it or she'll murder me. She wears it to almost every football game because she says it brings the team good luck."

I hug the sweatshirt to my chest. "A lucky cheerleading hoodie! This is *exactly* what I need to be a poppy! But if Jazmin sees me with it, she will know you took it."

Bea thinks for a moment. "Turn it inside out. Then she won't know it's her sweatshirt. You can wear it today. Maybe some of the luckiness will rub off. I'll sneak it back into her room tonight."

I beam at my clever friend. "Bea," I say, "you are a genius!"

Bea tilts her hips and does a sassy smile. "Tell me something I don't know," she replies. "Try it on. Let's see how it looks on you."

I do as Bea suggests, turning the hoodie fuzzy side out and wriggling it on, over my head. Jazmin is bigger than me, so the sleeves hang over my hands. The bottom of the sweatshirt almost touches my knees.

I do a supermodel pose. "How do I look?" I ask Bea.

Bea crinkles her eyebrows, studying me for a moment. "A little goofy," she replies honestly.

"I don't mind looking goofy as long as it makes me lucky," I say, rolling up the inside-out sweatshirt sleeves. Then I step back and try another cartwheel.

"Hey!" Bea cries when I finish. "That one was pretty good! Your arms were much straighter, but your knees were still bent. Here, eat this. It might help."

Bea pulls a zippy bag from her backpack and holds it out to me. It's filled with little brown pellets.

I wrinkle my nose, examining the bag of pellets like a cautious hamster. Then I unzip the bag and take a sniff. "Is this . . . *oatmeal*?" I ask my BFF.

Bea nods. "Technically, steel-cut oats. But yes, when you cook them, what you've got is basically . . . oatmeal."

I make a disgusted face. *Yuck.* If oatmeal friended me, I would *un*friend it immediately. I dislike it more than burned popcorn. More than creepy spiders. More than dog slobber. More than Annelise. "How is *oatmeal* going to help me be a better cheerleader?" I ask.

"Jazmin is into healthy food," Bea explains. "She eats steel-cut oats for breakfast every morning. Cooked, of course, but I didn't want them to go bad in my backpack, so yours are fresh out of the box!" Bea smiles, like this is good news.

I do *not* want to eat steel-cut oats. But I *do* want to be a cheerleader. If eating them will help, I'll give it a try.

I pour some of the pellets into my hand. "Yum," I say, nibbling a few like the middle-sized Billy Goat Gruff. I work them around, chewing my cud.

"How do they taste?" Bea asks a moment later. "Good?"

I spit oats onto the grass. *"Baaad,"* I reply and hand the bag back to Bea.

Bea slumps. "Darn," she says, zipping the bag shut. "Jazmin says eating healthy makes her a better cheerleader. Steal-cut oats are about as healthy as you can get."

"Sis, boom, *blah*," I say. "I want to be a cheerleader

and be healthy, but I *can't* eat those." I brush a pellet off my sweatshirt. "I'll stick with the hoodie for now. I'm sure if I wear it all day it will bring me good luck at practice tonight *and* at tryouts next week!"

We start practicing cartwheels again, more determined than ever to do them perfectly.

"How's practice going, you two?" someone asks a few minutes later.

Bea and I look toward the sidewalk. Jazmin is walking by with her friends. Bea must have told her we were meeting early to practice.

Jazmin gives my baggy, inside-out sweatshirt the once over. But she doesn't say anything about it, so she must not realize it belongs to her. *Whew!*

"Good," Bea tells her sister, as she adjusts her ponytail. "Except that cartwheels make me feel *queasy*. And Vicka's knees have a *serious* case of the bends."

"Show me what you've got," Jazmin says, walking over to us as her friends head inside the school.

"Okay," I say, even though I'm exhausted and the day has barely begun.

I do a cartwheel for Jazmin.

My sweatshirt sags.

My knees bend.

My ponytail flops.

"Good try!" Jazmin says encouragingly.

"You're getting better," Bea adds. "Really! Your legs only bent a little that time."

"But *better* isn't good enough," I say. "I have to be the *best*!"

"There's only one way to do that," Jazmin says. "Practice!"

"But I only have until next week," I reply, putting my glasses back on again. My discouragement is getting the best of me. "I could practice night and day, but I still won't be as good as Annelise. Her cartwheel is perfect. Plus, she can do the splits! When I try to do them, I fall — *splat!* — on the ground."

"Cheerleading is about more than cartwheels and

the splits. It's about school spirit and teamwork too!" Jazmin says.

"That's what I've been trying to tell her," Bea chimes in.

Jazmin thinks for a moment, checking the time. Then her eyes brighten with an idea. "Meet me by the football bleachers during lunch hour," she says.

I perk up. "Are you going to teach me how to do a perfect cartwheel?" I ask.

"And the splits?" Bea wonders.

"No," Jazmin replies. "I'm going to teach you how to do something even *better.*"

Bea and I gawk at each other. Then we turn to Jazmin. "What is it?" we ask anxiously.

Jazmin leans in.

"I'm going to teach you my *secret weapon!*"

Chapter 5

The Secret Weapon

Bea and I inhale our lunches and then bolt for the cafeteria door. Jazmin told us to meet her by the football field bleachers, which are all the way across the school's courtyard and halfway down the football field sideline. We will have to run if we're going to have time to learn her secret weapon before the bell rings for our next class.

"What do you think the secret weapon will be?" I ask Bea as we zigzag past tables and hungry kids who are entering the Caf.

"No idea," Bea replies. "But I hope it involves pom-poms! They are the only part of cheerleading I like!"

I smile at my best friend. She loves glittery things. Hair bands and barrettes. Bracelets. Notebooks. Even her orange backpack shimmers like a giant bike reflector when the sun hits it just right. And you should see Bea's bedroom. She decorated the walls with sparkly butterfly decals, and the ceiling is speckled with glow-in-the-dark stars! My room has some sparkle too, but not nearly as much as Bea's. And my orange backpack doesn't shimmer in the sunshine. Right now, the Muskrat's blue and gold pompoms are the glitteriest things around! If I can shine half as much as them, I will be a poppy for sure!

"Where are you *monkeys* off to in such a hurry?" someone asks. "Going back to the *zoo*?"

I look over and see Annelise getting in line for her food. Grace and Katie are right behind her. Why does Annelise always show up just when we are in the middle of important cheerleading business?

"Nowhere," I reply.

"Yeah, nowhere," Bea adds.

"Nowhere, huh?" Annelise says, stepping in and blocking our path just as we are about to zip out the door. "That sounds like a fun place. Grace will go with you."

Grace blinks with surprise. "I will?"

"Yes," Annelise answers. "And when you get back, tell me all about nowhere, got it?"

Grace frowns. But then she nods.

"But what about lunch?" I ask. "Grace hasn't eaten yet."

"She can eat on the way," Annelise says, pointing to the lunch box Grace is carrying. "Katie will save her a brownie."

"I will?" Katie asks.

"Yes," Annelise replies. "You will."

I don't have time to discuss brownies or argue with Annelise. We were supposed to meet Jazmin five minutes ago! What if she decides we're not coming, gets mad, and leaves. She might decide not to show us the secret weapon after all.

"Report back to me before our next class," Annelise says to Grace as she takes a food tray. "I'll save you a brownie too."

Grace smiles. Then she sneezes — *Achoo!* — right on Annelise's tray!

"Sorry!" Grace says. "My fall allergies are acting up."

Annelise scowls at her sneezed-on tray. Then she trades it with Katie's.

I take off down the hallway.

Bea and Grace follow along.

"Is nowhere outside?" Grace asks, sneezing again.

"Yes," I reply, even though I'm not exactly sure where nowhere is now. I can't lead Grace to Jazmin. Annelise already thinks we are practicing for tryouts. I don't want her to know we are doing more than practicing. We are getting a secret weapon!

"Ugh," Grace says, wiping her nose on a tissue. "My allergies are driving me crazy."

"It's not too late to turn back," I say. I push the

courtyard door wide open, hoping Grace will decide the outside air is too sneezy for her.

I step outside and hold the door for Bea. She steps outside too.

We turn and look at Grace who is tossing her tissue into a trash can. She hesitates, but then steps outside too. "Annelise will be mad if I don't go with you, and I know what she does to people she's mad at. I'd rather sneeze."

Fortunately, Grace is so busy blowing her nose and trying to eat her lunch on the go, she doesn't ask what we're up to. *Un*fortunately, she hangs with us for the entire of lunch break. I don't dare go near the football field for fear Jazmin will see us and wave us over. Then I'll have to explain to Grace why we're meeting with her, and she will report back to Annelise.

So instead, I lead Bea and Grace on a wild goose chase around the courtyard. First we wander around the patio tables. Next we examine the shrubbery. Finally we walk in circles around the flagpole. I keep hoping Grace will get bored and head back to the cafeteria for her brownies, but she stays stuck to us like a pesky burr. When the bell rings, we have no choice but to head back inside the school for afternoon classes.

"So where did they take you?" I overhear Annelise ask when we get back to our lockers.

"Nowhere," Grace replies, taking two brownies from a napkin on the palm of Annelise's hand.

Annelise crumples the napkin in her fist. "Then what did they do?"

"Nothing," Grace says, lifting a brownie to her mouth.

Annelise scowls and snatches the brownie away before Grace can take a bite. "No info, *no* brownies," she says. Then she snags the other one too. She takes a big bite out of it, turns around, and marches away in her sparkly shoes.

Katie and Grace follow a few steps behind her, hunched together, whispering to each other.

I latch my locker door, whirl the com so it locks, and hurry into our classroom with Bea.

❀ ❀ ❀

I'm so worried that Jazmin will be upset with us for ditching her that I can't concentrate on my history chapter. Mrs. Larson is letting us take turns reading it aloud. When it's my turn to read, Bea has to nudge my back with a pencil to get me to snap out of my worrying. Then she has to point out where we left off in the chapter. Mrs. Larson does not look pleased.

I'm distracted during phys ed too. Twice, Drew clobbers me in Poison Ball. "Earth to Vicka!" he shouts just before clobbering me for a third time. "You're not even *trying* to get away!"

"My mind is somewhere else today," I reply.

Drew does a goofy grin. He hugs the poison ball like it's a puppy. "*Awww . . .*" he says, "Were you thinking about *me*?"

I shake my head. "No," I say, distracted.

Drew's goofy grin fades. "Then what — *oof!*"

Henry clobbers Drew with a poison ball!

"You snooze, you lose!" Henry shouts then dashes away, laughing.

Drew is out of the game!

"Thanks a *lot*, Vicka," he says, shuffling off the gym floor.

Great. First Jazmin is mad at me. And now my crush is too! So far, sixth grade is *unfortunately complicated*!

Chapter 6

Do The Wave!

As soon as we get to cheerleading practice after school, we rush to find Jazmin and explain to her why we didn't show up during lunch hour.

"That's okay!" Jazmin says. "I figured something came up. We'll practice later."

I'm relieved Jazmin isn't mad at me. Bea and I join the other girls who are there for practice. Annelise, Katie, and Grace are sitting on the bleachers, talking. They talk a lot. Especially before, *during*, and after classes. All three have their hair pulled back in bouncy ponytails, just like Bea and me, only they must keep brushes and hairspray in their lockers because their ponytails are sleek and glittery, not bunched up and straggly like ours. (Note to self: Bring a locker mirror and hair supplies to school!) They are even wearing blue and gold Muskrat hoodies — *right* side out — and matching fingernail polish. They already look like real cheerleaders and practice hasn't even started!

"How will I ever beat Annelise, Katie, and Grace?" I ask Bea.

"You don't have to beat them," Bea says matter-of-factly.

"I don't?"

Bea shakes her head. "All you have to do is get the *fourth* spot."

I hadn't thought about it like that before. I don't have to beat everyone. I just have to be in the top four!

I look around at the other girls. Some of them look as nervous as me. One of them is doing backflips along the sideline. Her name is Jenny. She moved to Middleton this summer.

"Wow, look at Jenny," I exclaim. "She'll get the fourth spot for sure!"

"No, she won't," Bea says. "Remember? Jazmin is going to teach us her secret weapon! That is sure to get you on the squad!"

Bea is right again. What would I do without my BFF? If I had just a *glimmer* of her confidence, I could outshine all the girls at tryouts!

Jazmin and the other older cheerleaders arrive, carrying a bunch of pompoms and a cooler of ice water. "Welcome to cheerleading practice!" Jazmin says. "Today, we will teach you the routine for tryouts. Everyone will do the same routine, but you can change it up to make it your own. We will be looking for lots of Muskrat creativity and school spirit!" She glances at me and smiles.

One of the nervous-looking girls raises her hand. "What about cartwheels? Will we have to do them too?"

I hear Annelise sniff a laugh. "Duh," she mumbles.

"It's true, we *will* be judging your athletic ability," Jazmin replies, "but school spirit and teamwork are just as important!"

Suddenly a loud horn blows from somewhere behind the Snack Shack. That's where the Booster Club sells popcorn and candy during football games. Everyone turns to look. The horn blows again.

Honk!

Out runs a furry, brown muskrat! Not a real muskrat. This is someone dressed up in our school's mascot costume, running around in circles like Lucas did when we were playing cat and rat the other day.

"Here comes my brother!" a cheerleader named Brianna shouts.

"That's Drew?" Bea asks.

Brianna nods. "I had to pay him *ten dollars* to wear that costume!"

All the older cheerleaders laugh. "What a nice brother!" one of them says.

"*Greedy* brother is more like it," Brianna jokes.

That's when I remember that Drew has an older sister named Brianna. Which means my crush is here, dressed up like a muskrat!

HONK!

"Go, Muskrats!" Drew shouts. Then he drops his horn and does a silly cartwheel that barely gets off the ground. Everyone laughs. When he tries to do the splits, he falls to the ground — *splat!* — just like me!

Everyone applauds as he jumps up and takes a clownish bow. Drew looks right at me from behind his muskrat mask, so I do a clownish curtsy in return. Everyone laughs again, including Drew! Then he tromps up and down the sidelines in his clunky muskrat boots, trying to get us to do The Wave.

"He's so funny!" Katie says as Drew waves his paws in the air and jumps up and down in his furry costume.

"And *cute!*" Grace says. "When he isn't wearing a mask, that is." She giggles and whispers something to Katie behind her hand. Katie giggles too and whispers something back.

Uh-oh, I think. *Does Grace like Drew too?*

"*Cute?*" Annelise wrinkles her nose. "More like *weird.* You couldn't pay me a million dollars to wear that goofy costume!"

I shrug. "I don't think it's so bad. And with all that fake fur, he'll keep warm at the football games!"

Annelise rolls her eyes and shakes her head. "I'm not surprised you would think wearing something that makes you look stupid is a good thing." She gives my lucky sweatshirt the once over. "Here's a fashion tip, Vicka. Wear clothes that *fit* you. And *don't* put them on inside out."

I ignore Annelise and turn to Bea. "I didn't know Drew was our school mascot," I say.

Jazmin glances over. "He's just helping out for today," she explains. "We'll be naming a new mascot after cheerleading tryouts."

"Why aren't you doing The Wave, Vicka?" Drew

asks, coming up to me. "Too busy thinking about me again?" He grabs my hands in his furry paws and lifts them over my head, snickering behind his grinning muskrat mask. Then he moves down the line until everyone is doing The Wave.

Fortunately, Drew's voice was muffled behind his mask, so hopefully the other girls didn't hear his comment. Plus, he doesn't seem to be mad at me for making him lose at Poison Ball. *Un*fortunately, I feel my cheeks blush and not because I'm wearing a big, hot sweatshirt. I've known Drew since kindergarten, and his teasing never bothered me before. But now that I have a crush on him, I turn red as a tomato when he catches me off guard with his jokes. Sometimes I wish I could go back in time. Friendships were easier when I was Lucas's age.

I fan my face, wishing the pompoms were within reach so I could hide behind them.

"What's the matter, monkey girl?" Annelise asks. "Your face is *red* and your *paws* look sweaty!"

Annelise gets Grace and Katie to laugh along at her joke. "Quick! Bring Vicka a cup of ice water!" she shouts at the girls who are standing near the water cooler. "I think she's lovesick!"

Katie and Grace laugh again with Annelise, but not as loudly or as long.

Bea sticks out her tongue at Annelise. It's a baby-ish thing to do, but I'm happy to have a friend who backs me up.

"Go, Muskrats!" Drew shouts again. Then he takes a final blow, blows his horn, and disappears behind the Snack Shack.

The cheerleaders call us over to the team bench where they begin handing out pompoms. Annelise rushes to the front of the pack, wanting the best pair.

Bea, Grace, Katie, and I follow along. "Why do you do that?" I ask Grace.

"Do what?" Grace asks.

"Laugh at Annelise's dumb jokes and agree with her, even when it seems like you don't want to?"

Grace glances at Katie. "We were nobodies until we started hanging out with Annelise," she explains. "As soon as she let us be her friends, things changed. Now we sit with the popular kids in the lunchroom. We get first dibs on the best basketballs at open gym. And she buys us candy and bracelets when we do stuff for her."

"She's paying you with candy and bracelets to be her friend?" I ask.

Katie shrugs. "Not always. Usually we have to bring the candy to her sleepovers."

"Some friend," Bea says.

"What does she make you do for her?" I ask.

Grace blows her stuffy nose before answering. "Get the dirt on people she doesn't like. Spy for her. Stuff like that."

Katie starts to say something, but Jazmin and the other cheerleaders have started teaching the tryout cheer and routine to everyone, so the four of us grab the last pompoms and pay attention.

S - U - C - C - E - S - S !
That's the way you spell success!
Let's go! The Muskrats are the best!
Let's go! The best of all the rest!
Let's go, let's go, let's go . . . YAY!

The cheer is easy. Bea and I have heard it before at football games. But the routine looks hard. There is a lot of jumping and arm waving and pompom shaking. Then, at the end, all the cheerleaders do a cartwheel that ends with the splits!

I look at Bea.

She looks at me.

"I'm doomed," I say.

Bea steels her jaw. "No, you're not," she says. "You are Victoria Torres, Cheerleader. We have all week to learn the routine. Plus, you are wearing a lucky hoodie. And don't forget . . ." Bea leans in. "Soon we'll have a *secret weapon*!"

Annelise glances over.

I hush Bea. "Not so loud," I say, "or you'll let the cat out of the bag!"

Chapter 7

Snap, Crackle, Hop!

The cheerleaders split up the group so they can help us practice the routine. Fortunately, I get paired with Bea. Jazmin is our leader.

*Un*fortunately, Annelise and her partner, Jenny, are practicing right next to us. I like Jenny, but she and Annelise are both very good cheerleaders. Already, they can do most of the jumps and claps their leader is teaching them. Both of them can even do cartwheels that end in the splits!

Watching them makes me feel less confident. Some of the other girls are watching too. When they compliment Jenny on her cartwheels, she offers them some tips. She's almost as good as the girl in the video Bea and I watched!

Annelise pulls Jenny away from the other girls. "Don't help them! *I* want to win at tryouts."

Jenny shakes off Annelise's grip. "I like helping everyone do their best."

Annelise puts her hands on her hips. "This is a competition. If you want to be my partner, then you have to play to win."

Jenny crosses her arms. "Guess what?" she says. "I *don't* want to be your partner."

Wow, Jenny really stood up to Annelise! I admire her confidence.

Jenny walks over to a group of girls who are practicing together. One of them, Tara, becomes Jenny's new partner. They start practicing the routine.

Annelise's mouth drops open. She's left standing alone for a change.

Marching over to Grace and Katie, who are laughing hysterically as they work on a tricky jump, she tells them, "I'm with you now. Stop goofing around. Let's get to work."

Grace and Katie stop laughing. Annelise takes over their routine.

"Hey, Victoria. Pay attention, please," Jazmin says. I look away from Annelise and the other girls.

"I'm sorry," I reply. "I'm just worried I won't do well at tryouts. I could really use that secret weapon you promised to teach us!"

Annelise glances over again. Seriously, I think she's part bat. She must have sonar the way she tunes in every time I don't want her to.

Bea nudges me. "*Shhh!*" she says. "Now *you're* letting the cat out of the bag!"

I shoot a glance at Annelise. But she's gone back to telling Grace and Katie what to do. Maybe her sonar isn't so strong after all.

"I'll teach you the Snap, Crackle, Hop! tomorrow," Jazmin says. "That's what I call the secret weapon. First, you need to learn the basics. Cheerleading takes a lot of energy. So let's get warmed up by running a lap around the football field!"

I'm not crazy about running around the football field. Neither is Bea. But if running laps is what it takes to be a poppy, I'll do it.

"Isn't this fun?" I say to Bea as we run past the twenty-yard line on our way to the end zone. I try to sound upbeat, like I have tons of school spirit, even though my spirit is sputtering and my glasses keep slipping down my sweaty nose.

"Fun like the *flu*," Bea replies, chugging along beside me. We round the corner, run all the way to the other end zone, then head down the long stretch to the bleachers where the other girls are shaking pompoms and shouting out the S-U-C-C-E-S-S! cheer.

S - U - C - C - E - S - S !
That's the way you spell success!

"T-I-R-E-D," Bea says as we tumble to the grass at our starting point. "That's the way you spell *exhausted*."

"How come we're the only ones running laps?" I ask Jazmin as I catch my breath.

"Because no one else wants to be cheerleaders as much as you!" Jazmin replies. "Now give me ten."

"Ten what?" Bea asks from where she is lying like a capital *X* on the grass. "Ten heart attacks?"

Jazmin laughs. "Ten *push-ups*! Then we'll practice cartwheels."

Bea and I groan. "Hello, 9-1-1?" I say. "Come quick. This is an emergency."

Jazmin crosses her arms and tilts her hips, just like Bea does sometimes. "Okay, make it *five* push-ups. But the better shape you are in, the brighter you'll shine at tryouts."

I manage to do four and a half push-ups.

Bea does three.

"Good job!" Jazmin says. "Time for cartwheels."

Jazmin is a great teacher, but no matter how hard I try, my cartwheels are wobbly and crooked. I clean the smudges off my glasses and look around at the other girls again. No one is as good as Annelise or Jenny, but everyone is better than me.

"Keep working," Jazmin tells us at the end of practice. "The judges like to see that you are trying hard and doing your best! Grab a drink before you go."

"I thought cheerleading was all about being popular," I say as Bea guzzles a cup of water from the cooler. "So far, it's all about *panting* and *sweating*!" I pull off my lucky cheerleading hoodie and hand it back to Bea so she can sneak it into Jazmin's bedroom before she notices it's missing.

Bea uses the hoodie to wipe her sweaty face. Then she nods in agreement with what I said. "And we haven't even gotten to shake a pompom yet!"

"You might as well give up now, Vicka," Annelise says, butting in front of me and filling a paper cup with water. She takes a sip. "You'll never beat me. And Jenny is almost as good. Grace and Katie aren't far behind." She crumples the cup and tosses it on the grass. "One, two, three, *four* . . ." she says, counting on her fingers. That's all the squad needs." She smirks and waves goodbye to me. "*Adios*, Vicka!"

❀ ❀ ❀

"How was cheerleading practice?" Mom asks when I get home.

"Great," I say, opening the refrigerator door and sticking my head inside, trying to cool off my sweaty face. "Couldn't be better." I don't want to tell Mom the truth — that almost everyone is a better cheerleader than me.

*Un*fortunately, I'm a terrible liar. Mom is frowning at me as I grab a tangerine and turn to face her.

"How was practice, really?" she asks.

I sigh and start peeling the tangerine. "Parts of it were fun — Drew dressed up in the school mascot costume and got us to do The Wave."

"That does sound fun," Mom says.

"But parts of it weren't so great," I continue. "Jazmin had Bea and I run laps and warm up before learning the cheer — that was tiring. Plus, my glasses kept slipping — that was annoying. And the cheer has some really hard parts. Annelise was there, bossing us around and saying there was no way Bea or I could beat her at tryouts."

"Vicka, you know that girls like Annelise build themselves up by putting other people down," Mom says. "They act bossy because it makes them feel more powerful. They think the only way to earn respect is by being a big shot. Annelise probably can't imagine anyone could like her if they knew her faults. She may be a good cheerleader, but she needs to learn how to be a good friend if she wants to succeed at the things that matter most. When she does, she'll find out that people will respect her for who she is on the inside, not for how she acts on the outside."

Mom takes a bowl down from a cupboard and gives it to me for my tangerine. "Don't put up with her bullying, but don't be mean in return. That only brings you down to the bully's level. Finish your snack, then help me get supper ready, okay?"

I nod and carry my snack to the living room. As I eat, I think about what Mom said. It's true, the only so-called friends Annelise has are the ones who let her boss them around so they can get things from her — popularity or candy or invitations to fancy parties. If all of us would stick together, instead of sticking to Annelise, there wouldn't be anyone left for her to boss around.

Chapter 8

Annebeast

The next day, Bea and I are too excited to wait until after school to learn the Snap, Crackle, Hop! so we track down Jazmin between classes and cross-our-heart-hope-to-die-stick-a-needle-in-our-eye promise to show up if she will meet with us during lunch.

"Okay," Jazmin agrees.

Later, at the Caf, we are extra careful to stay away from Annelise. When she walks in, we ditch our trays at the dish room window and quickly leave by a different door.

Bea glances back at Annelise as we slip away. "Katie and Grace aren't with her today. Weird."

"Maybe they're tired of feeling like glue sticks," I suggest.

Despite the chilly fall breeze, we are panting like racehorses when we finally trot up to Jazmin, who is waiting for us on the football field bleachers.

"Good!" Jazmin says, popping out her earbuds and hopping down from the bleachers onto the grassy football field. "I was hoping you'd run here. Cheerleaders need to be in good shape!"

"All I really need is to be popular," I say, catching my breath.

Jazmin makes a face. "Pompoms won't make you popular, Vicka."

Bea nudges me. "That's what I've been trying to tell you," she says.

Deep down, I know Jazmin and Bea are right. But it still seems like being a cheerleader would help me shine brighter in the popularity department. I think about Jenny and how great she was at practice yesterday. She was even teaching moves to the other girls. Everyone thanked her afterward. I want to shine like that too!

"Will you teach us the secret weapon now?" I ask Jazmin.

Jazmin smiles. "Sure," she says. "It's a fancy move I learned at cheerleading camp this summer. I was saving it for our first football game, but I'll let you two use it for tryouts. Like I said, it's called the Snap, Crackle, Hop!"

I give Jazmin a big smile. "Thank you! The Snap, Crackle, Hop! is exactly what I need to win a spot on the squad!"

Jazmin laughs. "You can't win a spot on the squad. You have to earn it. Only hard work and practice will do that. But I know you've got what it takes!"

I don't feel as confident as Jazmin seems to be. I watch carefully as she performs the S-U-C-C-E-S-S! cheer. Then, at the end, she *snaps* her legs in a scissors kick, claps her hands in a *crackling* rhythm, and ends with a twirling *hop*.

"Go, Muskrats!" Jazmin shouts.

"Wow, that looks harder than a cartwheel!" I say.

Bea nods in agreement. "Even harder than the splits!"

"But it's not," Jazmin says. "I'll break it down. Watch."

Jazmin does the fancy move again, more slowly. "Just *kick . . . clap . . . hop.* Now you try."

Bea and I give the Snap, Crackle, Hop! our best shot. At least my glasses stay put, but even in slow motion it's hard to do well.

"I think our secret weapon should be called the Slump, Crumple, Flop," I say, after a few attempts.

"Don't get discouraged," Jazmin says. "Keep practicing! You'll get it!"

Jazmin heads back to the school building. Bea and I keep practicing until the bell rings for afternoon classes. "We better hurry, or we'll be late for history again," Bea says, pulling me along. "Two tardies and Mrs. Larson will give us detention!"

We zoom around the far end of the bleachers so fast we almost crash into the Snack Shack. Then we nearly tackle Grace and Katie who, for some strange reason, are lurking behind it.

❀ ❀ ❀

Fortunately, we get to history class in the nick of time. *Un*fortunately, the assignment board has a big message written on it:

Chapter 1 Quiz Tomorrow!

I write a reminder in my student planner. Turning around in my chair, I ask Bea, "Do you want to study for our quiz after cheerleading practice?"

"Can't," Bea replies. "Mom is picking us up. I have piano lessons, and Jazmin has an orthodontist appointment. We'll be busy until after supper."

"Darn" I say. "I could use your help studying. I have to do well if I'm going to be a cheerleader."

"You'll have to do well, when you are a cheer-leader," Bea says confidently. "You could ask someone else to study with you tonight."

I look around the classroom.

Some of the boys are flicking paper triangle foot-balls across their desks. Annelise is passing notes with Grace and Katie. Jenny is reading the assignment board and writing notes in her student planner.

Maybe Jenny would want to study with me? She's nice. I wonder if she is as good at history as she is at backflips.

Even though Mrs. Larson does not allow note passing during class, she's helping Henry fix a torn page in his textbook. I'll have time to pass a note to Jenny before Mrs. Larson notices. Quickly, I tear a piece of paper from my notebook.

Jenny,
study for our quiz?
With me?
After practice?
~Vicka

I fold the note up and write Jenny's name on the outside. Then I pass it down the aisle. Fortunately, it makes its way to the back of the row and then across the aisle speedy-quick. *Un*fortunately, Annelise sees what's going on just as Mrs. Larson tells us to open our books to today's chapter. Annelise snatches the note, opens it, and starts reading what I've written!

I want to yell, "STOP!" but then Mrs. Larson would know I'm passing notes during class.

Anne*beast* folds up the note again, then raises her hand. "Mrs. Larson," she says, waving my note like a warning flag. "Some kids are passing notes over here!"

Then the beast glances at me and grins.

I narrow my eyes and imagine laser beams shooting out of them.

Mrs. Larson takes the note from Annelise, reads the name written on the outside of it, and says, "Jenny, you know the rules. Please save the socializing for after class."

Jenny's eyes go wide. "But I wasn't passing notes!"

"Your name is written on this one," Mrs. Larson says, tucking the note into her blazer pocket. "See me after class."

Jenny's shoulders slump.

Silently, I sink into my chair. My face heats up like a stewed tomato. Getting teased isn't the only thing that can make your blush. So can getting into trouble with your teacher and letting a classmate take the heat for it.

"By the way, Annelise," Mrs. Larson continues, turning to her, "while it is true that I don't allow note passing during class, I imagine it is also true that your classmates don't appreciate tattling. I suggest you think twice before taking your friendships for granted."

Now Annelise sinks into *her* chair. Her face turns tomato red too.

As Mrs. Larson begins our lesson, I sneak a glance at Jenny.

She is staring straight ahead at the marker board as Mrs. Larson writes on it. I barely know Jenny, and now I've gotten her into trouble for something she didn't even do!

When class is over, I don't even wait for Bea. I rush out of the classroom as fast as I can. Then I spend the rest of the day avoiding Jenny.

When I get home from school, I practice the Snap, Crackle, Hop! in my backyard. My secret weapon is still more of a *flop* than a *hop*. But like Jazmin said, all I can do is keep practicing.

Sofia is in the kitchen having a snack when I get inside.

"My first quiz of middle school is tomorrow," I tell her. "Will you help me study for it? I have to do well or my poppy dreams are over."

Sofia munches on trail mix and squints at me. "Why would you dream of being a flower?"

I roll my eyes. "Not *that* kind of poppy," I reply. "*Poppy* as in popular? Cheerleading is my only chance to really shine, but if I don't get good grades, I can't be on the squad."

Sofia shakes her head. "You should study to be smarter, not to be more popular."

"Uh-huh," I reply, nibbling some of Sofia's trail mix. There's one thing I've learned in my unfortunately average life: agreeing with your older sister makes things much easier. "Will you help me study anyway?"

"Nope," Sofia says, pouring trail mix into a container. "I'm meeting Deon at her house in a few minutes. We're study buddies this year."

"Who's Deon? And what's a study buddy?" I ask.

"Just what it sounds like," Sofia replies. "A *buddy* who *studies* with you. Deon and I have math together, so we're going to meet at each other's house, once a week, to study together."

"Cool," I say.

"Of course it's cool," Sofia says. "Being a *smarty* is way cooler than being a *poppy*." She tosses the trail mix into her backpack and heads out the door.

I grab my history book and hop up onto a stool by the counter. Sofia is right. Being smart is important. I open my textbook and start rereading our chapter.

But the whole time I read, I scissors kick my legs under the counter.

Later, while I review my glossary words, I clap in rhythm as I read each definition.

And when I fill in the blanks on the review work-sheet Mrs. Larson gave us, I butt-hop as I complete each one.

By the time I get to Mrs. Larson's classroom the

next day, I am feeling ready for the quiz. I'm still feeling embarrassed about getting Jenny into trouble yesterday, but I managed to avoid her in the hallways and lunchroom all morning. As soon as I'm done with my history quiz, I zip away without speaking to her. And since it's Friday, we don't have cheerleading practice after school. Hooray! Maybe she'll forget all about the note passing before I see her again on Monday.

Chapter 9

Say The Magic Word

Fortunately, it's Saturday. Bea and I will have all weekend to practice the Snap, Crackle, Hop! *Un*fortunately, the rest of my routine still isn't the best. But our secret weapon is sure to catch the judges by surprise. Hopefully, it will be enough to get me on the squad so I can finally shine! Tryouts are only a few days away!

I've been practicing the routine so much, all I can think about is cheerleading. I was thinking about it when I didn't hear teachers call on me during class yesterday — three times. *Yikes.* Then, at supper, I squeezed ketchup on my ice cream instead of chocolate sauce. *Yuck*. Last night, I even dreamed Annelise and I were cheerleading partners. *Weird*. We got along great and *both* made the squad! Isn't that the craziest dream ever?

"Vicka!" Mom shouts just now as I pour cornflakes into Poco's food bowl instead of dog food.

Poco sniffs the cornflakes, then blinks his big, buggy eyes at me. "*Yip*?" he barks.

"*¡Uf!*" I say. "Sorry, Poco ol' pal."

Mom takes the cereal box from me before I can do more damage. "Where is your mind lately? You've been distracted for days."

"I've been thinking about cheerleading," I reply, emptying Poco's bowl into the compost bucket and refilling it with dog chow. Poco digs in, wagging his tail like a mini–windshield wiper. "I'm worried I won't be good enough to make the squad."

"All you can do is your best," Mom says.

"But my best is only average. I have to be above average if I'm going to be a poppy."

Mom gives me a blank look. "If you're going to be a what?"

"A *poppy*," I say again. "You know, *popular*. Then I will really shine in middle school!"

"Victoria Torres," Mom says, "being on the cheerleading squad won't make you popular. Only being you can do that."

"That's what Jazmin said too. But she is popular. She doesn't know what it's like to be just me, Victoria Torres, unfortunately average."

"You are exceptionally kind, generous, and friendly," Mom says. "There's nothing average about you, Vicka."

"Uh-huh," I say, patting Poco on the head after he finishes his breakfast. He licks his chops and wags his tail happily.

Just like with Sofia, agreeing with Mom is usually easier than disagreeing with her. I love my parents, but it's harder to get my way with Mom than it is with Dad. I've learned it's best to agree as much as possible with her and save up the disagreeing for when you really need it.

The phone rings. I answer it.

"Hi, it's me," Bea says. "Are you ready to meet at the park?"

"Ready or not, park, here I come," I reply.

Poco starts barking excitedly as soon as he hears me say the word *park*. He dances around my feet like a giant jumping bean. Then he races over the front door where his leash hangs on a hook.

Poco loves going for walks at the park. But today Bea and I are practicing for cheerleading. I walk over to Poco and pat his head again. "Sorry, Poco," I say. "I'm too busy to take you for a walk today."

Poco stops dancing. His tail droops. His ears sag.

Lucas looks over from the couch. He's eating cereal out of the box and watching cartoons on TV. "Did you say you're going to the park?" he asks, sitting up.

"Um," I say, not wanting to lie but also not wanting to take along my little brother. Lucas loves going to the park as much as Poco does. Unfortunately, he doesn't come with a leash.

"Yes, she did," Mom answers for me as she carries a laundry basket past me on her way to the washing machine. "Get your shoes on, Lucas."

"Yay!" Lucas cries, hopping off the couch and ditching the cereal box. He scrambles to find his sneakers.

I lean against the wall. "*¡Uf!*" I sigh.

❁ ❀ ❁

Bea is waiting for me by the jungle gym at the Middleton Park playground when I pull up on my bike a few minutes later. Fortunately, it's a warm, sunny day — we can practice cheerleading all morning! *Un*fortunately, Mom made me bring Lucas along.

"Don't wander off," I tell my little brother. "Stay on the wood chips."

"Yeah, yeah," Lucas says, dropping his bike and running toward the twisty slide where some friends are playing. "I'm not a *preschooler*, you know!"

"Oh, yay, you brought Lucas!" Bea says, "He's so sweet. I wish I had a little brother."

"Sometimes he's sweet," I say, watching as Lucas and two of his buddies race to the tire swing that's next to the twisty slide. All three climb on and get it to sway in lazy circles. "But sometimes he is really annoying." I pick up his bike and park it in the rack next to mine.

"Vicka!" Lucas calls to me. "Spin us!"

All three boys start chanting, "Spin! Spin! Spin!"

"See what I mean?" I say to Bea. "Just when I want to practice cheerleading, I have to take care of him."

We start to walk over to the tire swing, where the boys are now shouting their chant so loudly other kids are looking over to see what all the fuss is about.

"Hold on to your horses!" I yell to them. "I'm coming!"

But then I freeze. "Great," I say to Bea. "Look who's here."

Annelise pulls up on her bike. Grace and Katie

brake to a stop behind her. "I'll give you a spin," Annelise sweetly tells the boys.

"Yay!" they shout. "Spin! Spin! Spin!"

Annelise climbs off her bike and starts spinning the tire swing.

At first, the boys squeal like happy spider monkeys. But the more they squeal, the faster Annelise spins them. Soon the squeals change to wails. The louder they wail, the more Annelise grins.

"Stop the world!" Lucas shouts a minute later. "I wanna get off!"

But Anne*beast* keeps spinning the swing. "You have to say the magic word," she tells Lucas.

"*Pleeeeease*, stop!" he shouts.

"That's not the magic word," Annelise replies. "Try again."

The boys start shouting every magic word they know.

"Abracadabra!"

"Hocus-pocus!"

"Mischief managed!"

"*Pretty* please, with sugar on top!"

But each time they shout a word, Annelise tells them it's not the right one.

"You better stop spinning them," Grace says in a worried voice. "They are starting to look seasick!"

"You're not the boss of me," Annelise tells her.

Grace huffs and takes a step back. So does Katie.

I march over and slow down the swing.

"Hey!" Annelise glares at me. "You didn't say the magic word!"

"*Chihuahua*," I reply, stopping the swing. "*That's* the magic word. Shall I spell it for you?"

Annelise crosses her arms and narrows her eyes. "Very funny," she says.

"Thanks, Vicka. You are the best big sister in the world," Lucas and the other boys climb off the swing. He points a wobbly finger at Annelise. "And *that* girl is the biggest *meanie* in the world!"

Lucas stumbles away with his friends.

I turn to Annelise. "Why don't you pick on some-one your own size?" I ask.

"I was just goofing around," she says. "*My* little brother loves when I spin him like that."

"Well, *mine* doesn't," I reply. "C'mon, Bea, I need to run off some steam."

Bea and I take a lap around the jungle gym, jog past the picnic shelter, and then walk along the path that circles the playground. When we get back to the tire swing, Annelise, Grace, and Katie are gone.

Good. Now we can practice our secret weapon.

Chapter 10

The Queen of Confidence

When Lucas and I get home from the park, Dad is raking leaves in the front yard. Lucas runs inside. I show Dad my cheerleading routine.

"That was great, Vicka!" he says, leaning against his rake as I finish with the Snap, Crackle, Hop! "We did that same S-U-C-C-E-S-S! cheer when I was your age."

"Really?" I say. "Mine still needs work."

"Anything worth doing does!" Dad replies.

"But tryouts are in three days. I could practice for three years, and I still wouldn't be as good as some of the other girls trying out for the squad." I'm thinking about Annelise and Jenny when I say this, but I don't mention their names to Dad.

"The only surefire way not to succeed is not to try," Dad says. He puffs up his chest and grins. "I didn't make the varsity football team by giving up!"

"*You* played football in high school?" As soon as I ask the question, I realize I sound just like Annelise, when she couldn't believe I was trying out for cheerleading. I wish I could take it back. I don't want to hurt Dad's feelings, like Annelise hurt mine.

But Dad doesn't seem to feel bad. He laughs off my comment. "*Si*, Bonita," he replies, nodding. Bonita is Dad's nickname for me. It means *pretty little one* in Spanish. I don't like it when he calls me that name in public, but at home it's okay. "But things didn't turn out quite as I had hoped. I wanted to be the quarterback — who doesn't? — but I wasn't built for it. Instead, the coach made me a line backer. I wasn't the star player on our team, but that didn't keep me from trying my hardest. In the process, I had fun, made friends, and felt good about cheering for the guys who *were* the star players. That's what's most important: working hard and being a good teammate, no matter your skill level."

I hadn't thought about how being on the cheerleading squad is the same as being on a sports team. All this time, I've been thinking about me. *Me* making the squad. *Me* being more popular. *Me* shining like the sun instead of glittering along with all the other stars in the speckled night sky. Teamwork is about helping each other do your best so the whole team succeeds, not just one person on it.

"Let me see that cheer again, Bonita," Dad says.

I step back, take a big breath, and do the cheer again. "S-U-C-C-E-S-S!" I shout. "That's the way you spell success!"

When I finish the routine, Dad puts his fingers to his mouth and whistles. "Atta girl! Keep doing it like you mean it! Confidence is key. When you have confidence, you can't lose. Even if you don't win the contest, Vicka, I will be proud of you for doing your best!"

Dad thinks I can shine at tryouts.

So does Mom.

And Bea.

It looks like *confidence* is the magic word.

When it comes to believing in yourself, Sofia is the Queen of Confidence. She isn't a poppy, but she is a total brain. Sofia will be able to help me have the confidence I need to do well at cheerleading tryouts!

Fortunately, Sofia is home studying today. *Un*fortunately, she doesn't like to be disturbed when she's studying. But tryouts are coming fast! If I don't polish up my confidence soon, I'll never shine in time.

I go upstairs to Sofia's bedroom. A sign is taped to her closed door.

POR FAVOR, NO MOLESTAR

"Please, do not disturb," I read, translating the sign from Spanish to English.

I knock on the door anyway.

No answer.

I knock harder.

Still no answer.

"Sofia?!" I shout, pounding on the door. "I need to talk with y—"

The door flies open. Sofia glares at me. She points to the sign on her door. "*¿No podes leer español?*"

"Yes," I reply, "I can read Spanish. But I need your help with a big problem."

Sofia crosses her arms. "Ask Mom," she says. "I'm studying."

"But this is a middle school problem, and it's been *eons* since she was in middle school. You *are* in middle school. That makes you a *primary source*. Please?"

Sofia rolls her eyes. She growls like an annoyed bear. But I can tell she is also impressed with my use of a brainy word like *eons*. And I'm certain she's pleased with the thought of being a primary source. She adores research.

Sofia checks the time on her chunky watch. "Five minutes," she says, stepping aside. "That's how much time you have to tell me about your problem."

"Only five minutes?!" I exclaim. "But I told you, this is a *big* problem!"

"Make that four minutes and fifty-four seconds," Sofia replies, looking at her watch again. "I suggest you get to the point."

I dart into Sofia's surgical suite. That's what I call her bedroom because she wants to be a surgeon someday and because it is the cleanest, neatest room in our house. Unlike my room, her bed is always made. Her desk is always organized. No comic books or dirty clothes are scattered on the floor.

"Cut to the chase," Sofia says, checking the time. "You've used up another twelve seconds just getting into the room. Make that thirteen seconds . . . four-teen, fifteen . . ."

"Okay, okay!" I start talking fast. "I want to be a cheerleader, but Dad says I need more confidence if I'm going to do well at tryouts. You are the most confident person I know. How do you do it? Please give me some advice."

Sofia stops counting. She stares blankly at me for a moment. "You are joking, right? I *can't* be the most confident person you know."

I nod. "You are smart, cute, and popular. You are always on the phone with your friends or joining clubs at school. Only confident people do stuff like that."

Sofia sits down hard on her bed. *Wump!* "Listen, Vicka," she says. "I am *not* that smart. I *don't* think of myself as cute. And I have *never* been part of the popular crowd."

"But that can't be true. You get straight As. You are always texting your friends. And that cute boy down the block — Joey Thimble — likes you."

Sofia laughs. "Joey Thimble doesn't know I exist,

Vicka. I have a few close friends, not a crowd. And I get good grades because I study all the time. I'm in math club and have a study buddy because math is my hardest subject, so I need all the help I can get." She shakes her head and laughs again. "If anyone has confidence around here it's *you*."

Now I sit down. *Wump!* "Me?"

Sofia nods. "I would never in a million *eons* try out for cheerleading. Seriously? Standing in front of a crowd makes my stomach feel like I just ate a whole platter of Abuela's extra-spicy enchiladas." Our grandmother makes the spiciest — and most delicious — food in our family.

I fall back on Sofia's bed feeling dizzy with confusion. If my braniac sister doesn't think she has self-confidence, how can I ever hope to? "I'm doomed," I say.

"You're not doomed," Sofia replies. "You have what it takes to be popular in middle school, Vicka, whether or not you make the cheerleading squad."

I sit up again. "I do?"

Sofia nods. "*Si*, you are smart . . ." she starts to say.

I shake my head. "I only get Bs on my report card."

"That's only because you don't study as much as I do. Plus, you are cute and you already have a great best friend. You'll be fine." Sofia checks her watch. "Time is up. *Adios*."

"But —" I protest as Sofia pulls me to my feet and steers me to her door.

"No buts," she says. "I have to study. You should too. Stop worrying about tryouts. You will do fine."

She nudges me into the hallway and starts to close her bedroom door. But then she stops and makes a puzzled face. "By the way, what makes you think Joey Thimble likes me?"

I shrug. "He's always watching you when we walk past his house. Once I saw him writing your initials with chalk on his driveway. He scribbled over it when he realized I was there."

Sofia shakes her head. "That's crazy."

"Boys usually are," I reply.

The door closes.

Wump!

Lucas darts out of his bedroom. "Mom!" he shouts. "Look what I made for Vic—!"

Lucas sees me and suddenly stops shouting. "Oh," he says. "I thought you were Mom."

"She's downstairs," I say. "What did you make?"

Quickly, he hides something behind his back. "Nothing," he says, and darts down the stairs.

I shake my head. "Sofia is right. We both live with a bunch of goofballs."

I look at Sofia's closed door again.

"Por favor, no molestar."

I am on my own.

Chapter 11

Touchdown!

Some people think history is boring because of all the names and dates to memorize. Okay, so that part can be a *little* boring, but the other stuff — the inventions, discoveries, wars, and everything — is super interesting because it all tells a story.

This week, in Mrs. Larson's history class, we are starting a new unit about the first space mission to the moon. I love space stuff! Maybe I will be an astronaut some day. Either that or a dolphin trainer. Or maybe both! Victoria Torres, Space Explorer/Dolphin Trainer!

"Today, I want you to work with a partner to

summarize a section of our chapter," Mrs. Larson says.

She starts assigning partners. "Tara and Henry . . . Drew and Min . . . Annelise and Bea . . ."

Poor Bea! She's stuck with Anne*beast*! At least there are only desks and chairs in the classroom — no tire swings. Bea will be safe from getting spun around like a top.

" . . . Vicka and Jenny . . ."

Gulp!

I've been avoiding Jenny since I got caught passing a note to her last week. I'm sure she's upset that I let her take the blame. Mrs. Larson even made her stay after class!

Now I'm her partner. It's time for me to stop avoiding my problem and say something about what happened . . . before I chicken out.

"I'm super sorry I got you into trouble with Mrs. Larson last week," I blurt out as Jenny slides her chair over to my desk. "Please don't be mad at me forever."

Jenny pauses, taking this in. Then she sits down next to me. "Thanks, but you didn't get me into trouble," she says. "And I'm not mad at you."

"But you must be mad," I say. "I'm the one who was passing notes, but you're the one Mrs. Larson kept after class. Did she give you detention?"

Jenny giggles. "No. She just wanted to give me the note back. After I read it, I tried to find you, to say we could study together, but every time I saw you — *poof!* — you disappeared." Jenny shrugs. "You stayed away from me at cheerleading practice too. I figured you changed your mind."

I shake my head. "I was afraid you were mad at me. I should have apologized right away."

Jenny smiles. "Friends?"

I smile too. "Friends."

"Is everything all right over here?" Mrs. Larson asks as she gives Jenny and me a worksheet.

"Yes," I reply.

"Everything's fine," Jenny adds.

"Good," Mrs. Larson says, smiling. "Now get busy." She moves down the aisle.

We huddle up and look over our assignment.

Read Chapter 1, Section 3. Summarize it for the class.

Jenny and I take turns reading our section, which is all about the rocket blasting off and landing on the moon. When we finish, Jenny says, "Instead of just telling the class about the astronauts blasting off, why don't we show them?"

"What do you mean?" I ask. "Act it out?"

Jenny nods excitedly. "I love putting on little skits with my friends . . . do you?"

"Y-E-S, yes!" I say loudly. I've been shouting cheers so much lately, my voice is stuck at high volume. "It's a great idea!"

Jenny and I do a high five.

Annelise glances over from across the aisle, where she and Bea are working together. "What's your great idea?" she asks.

I clamp my hand over my mouth. *¡Uf!* It was Jenny's idea, not mine. She should be the one to let the cat out of the bag.

"It's a surprise," Jenny says to Annelise.

I nod. "Wait and see."

Annelise frowns. "I hate surprises. Tell me now."

Jenny thinks for a moment. "Here's a hint." She starts counting down. "Ten . . . nine . . . eight . . . seven . . . six . . . !"

"Five . . . four . . . three . . . two . . . one . . . !" I continue.

"Blast off!" we both shout, raising our hands in the air like we are leading a cheer at a football game.

Annelise scowls. Then she looks across the room at our teacher. "Mrs. Larson!" she calls. "Vicka and Jenny are being too noisy. Please tell them to work quietly."

"We are in charge of the blast off," I explain when Mrs. Larson walks over to us. "That's the noisiest parts of the astronauts' mission, and we want to act it out!" I clamp my hand over my mouth again. *¡Uf!*

"You're acting out your section?" Annelise asks.

I nod and uncover my mouth. "It was Jenny's great idea."

Annelise huffs. "Anyone can think of that."

"Perhaps you two would like to work in the hall-way?" Mrs. Larson asks Jenny and me. "Then you won't disturb your classmates, and you'll have more room to practice."

Jenny and I gather up our things. I hate to leave Bea behind, but sometimes even best friends have to get along without each other.

"I'm sorry I told Annelise your skit idea," I tell Jenny when we are out the door.

"That's okay," Jenny says. "I would have spilled it, if you hadn't. I'm bad at keeping secrets!"

A minute later, we are practicing our skit. Jenny is fun to work with. We are laughing the whole time. When we land on the moon, Jenny shouts, "Touchdown!" and falls to the floor, like she just landed in a moon crater!

"Touchdown!" I shout, raising my arms in the air like the referee at a football game.

"That's funny!" Jenny says. "Let's do that for the class."

When Mrs. Larson calls us back into the room, we are ready. First, Drew and Min summarize Section 1, which is all about mission control where the scientists work on their computers, keeping track of the rocket before, during, and after the space mission. It's an interesting summary, but they don't act it out. Jenny and I exchange a secret smile. Our skit will be more entertaining!

"Who has Section 2?" Mrs. Larson asks as Drew and Min return to their desks.

"We do, Mrs. Larson," Annelise says, marching to the front of the classroom. Bea follows along, shooting a worried glance at me. I can tell something is wrong. Usually Bea is eager to present things to the class. Maybe she's just bummed, getting stuck with Annelise.

"Our section is all about the astronauts training for their mission," Annelise says. "Instead of telling you about it, which would be boring . . ." she pauses to glance at Drew and Min, "we are going to *act it out!*" Annelise shoots a deadly grin at Jenny and me.

We gasp. Annelise *stole* our skit idea! By the look on Bea's face, I can tell this was all Annelise's doing.

Annelise and Bea pretend to enter a chamber called the flight simulator. They push invisible buttons, then begin spinning around, faster and faster. Poor Bea is getting spun by Annelise after all!

Suddenly they stop spinning. Annelise leans over and pretends to throw up! Bea does too, even though I can tell she doesn't want to.

"*Eww!*" Min says, making a disgusted face.

Some kids laugh. Henry and Sam applaud. Annelise smiles, soaking up the attention. She takes a bow and then pretends to throw up again! Drew just shakes his head.

"Welcome to Barfdom!" Henry shouts.

Mrs. Larson frowns. "That's enough, Henry." She turns to Annelise and Bea. "Please take your seats," she says, crisply.

Annelise high-fives Henry on the way to her desk. But Bea shuffles down the row quickly, ducking her head. "I'm sorry!" she whispers to me as she passes by. "It wasn't my idea to do a skit!"

Mrs. Larson calls on Jenny and me to present Section 3.

"We planned a skit too," Jenny says.

"Copycats," Annelise mumbles.

I scowl at Annelise. "But we promise not to get sick," I say.

Min sighs with relief.

Drew grins and nods.

"Excellent," Mrs. Larson says. "We've had enough of that for one day."

Annelise sits back in her chair and crosses her arms.

I smile.

Jenny and I perform our skit. At the end we shout, "Touchdown!" and raise our arms in the air, just like we planned.

Drew leads the class in a round of applause. He even puts his fingers to his mouth and whistles loudly, just like Dad can do!

Annelise does not clap or whistle. "That was dumb," she says. "A touchdown on the moon isn't the same as a touchdown at a football game."

"It was a clever play on words," Mrs. Larson says. "Good job, girls!"

Jenny and I hurry back to our desks, smiling. Mrs. Larson liked our skit!

"That was great, Vicka," Drew says from across the aisle. He smiles and holds out his hand for a high five.

"Thanks!" I reply, smacking the palm of his hand with mine, like we are old friends. Sometimes when things go your way, you feel invincible. Nothing can scare you, not even your crush! I feel like I can do anything now. Maybe even win at tryouts!

After everyone presents their summaries, Mrs. Larson hands back our graded chapter quizzes from last week. "This was your first quiz, so I'm pleased with how well most of you did." She catches my eye and smiles as she sets my quiz on my desk.

I look at the grade written on it.

B+ Above average! Sofia was right. Studying hard really does make you smarter.

"But a few of you will need to step up your game," Mrs. Larson adds as she hands back more quizzes.

I glance across the aisle as Annelise looks at her quiz. I catch a glimpse of an *F* written on it before she quickly turns the paper over.

Annelise *failed* our first quiz! I guess she isn't as good at studying as she is at cartwheeling. I'm not the best student in class either, but I do try my best. I take notes, and I turn in my homework on time. I study for quizzes. Annelise has never tried hard to be a good student. Last year, she joked about getting poor grades. She acted like she didn't care. But she'll have to do better if she hopes to be on the squad. Cheerleaders have to get good grades. That's one of the squad rules. If you fail in your classes, you fail as a cheerleader.

The bell rings and everyone gets up to leave. I drop my pencil. It rolls under Drew's desk. When he stands up, he accidentally-on-purpose kicks it down the aisle! Did he do it to be mean or was he teasing me again? Sometimes, with boys, it's hard to tell the difference.

I scurry after my pencil, which has rolled under a cart at the back of the classroom. As I kneel down to reach under the cart, I hear Mrs. Larson say, "Annelise? May I speak with you for a moment?"

I look toward the door. Everyone has filed out, except for Mrs. Larson and Annelise. They don't know I'm still in the room. I freeze.

"I must say, I was disappointed with your first quiz score," Mrs. Larson says to Annelise. "You are a bright girl. I know you can do better."

"It's not *my* fault!" Annelise protests. "You didn't tell us there would be a quiz!"

Mrs. Larson points to the marker board at the front of our classroom. That's where she writes the weekly schedule, including our homework assignments and upcoming quizzes. "We will have a quiz every Friday. I give you time at the start of class to make note of assignments. But I've noticed you are often talking with Grace or passing notes to Katie, instead of checking the board."

Annelise ducks her head. What Mrs. Larson said is true. Annelise is always chatting before class.

"Middle school is more difficult than elementary school," Mrs. Larson continues, as she and Annelise step out into the hallway. "The only way to succeed here is to be organized, study more, and try harder."

That makes me think of our cheer for tryouts.

S-U-C-C-E-S-S! That's the way you spell success!

It looks like Annelise needs another spelling lesson!

When Bea and I get to the football field for our last practice before tryouts tomorrow, we set our backpacks on the team bench and do the stretches Jazmin taught us.

"Mind if I join you?" Jenny asks, coming up to us.

"The more the merrier!" I say.

Jenny starts doing the stretches. Soon other girls arrive and join in. We all take a lap around the football field together.

"Warming up is more fun with lots of people," I say to Bea as we jog along.

"Agreed," Bea replies. "It *almost* makes me want to be on the squad."

"Who knows?" I say. "You might be the one to beat me!"

We slow to a stop. "That will never happen," Bea says. "But if I *did* make the squad and you didn't, I'd give up my spot for you. Cheerleading means more to you than it does to me."

I give Bea a hug. "You are the best BFF ever."

"I know," Bea says with a teasey grin. Then she hugs me back.

"What's with the hug fest?"

We turn to see Annelise walking up to us.

"Bea was wishing me good luck at tryouts," I reply.

Annelise snorts a laugh. "You'll need it," she says. Then she does a cartwheel to show off.

Bea narrows her eyes. "Friends stick together," she snaps. "If you had any friends, you'd know that."

Annelise scowls at Bea. Her eyes brighten with angry tears. "I have friends," she says. "But it takes more than that to be a cheerleader." She gives me an icy glare. "How is your *fall-apart* wheel coming along, Vicka?" She does a half-bent cartwheel, then walks off, laughing to herself. But I notice she is also wiping a tear from her eye.

"Don't listen to her," Bea says. "Being a cheerleader isn't just about doing cartwheels and cheering for the team. It's about cheering for each other too. You will do great!"

Chapter 12

Tryouts Tuesday

Tryouts are after school today! Fortunately, my scissors kick is very *snappy*. My clapping *crackles* with rhythm. And my fancy *hop* would make the Easter Bunny jealous. My glasses are squeaky clean, and even my ponytail sparkles! Jazmin let Bea and me borrow some of her glittery hairspray.

I look in my bedroom mirror and give myself a confident smile. Then I bite my lip. On the *outside*, I shine with confidence like the girl in the cheer video. But on the *inside*, I feel like Poco during a thunderstorm — quivering so much his toenails tap out a Morris Code message on the kitchen floor. *SOS!*

There is a knock on my bedroom door. My brother peeks in. "I made something for you, Vicka!"

"What is it?" I ask.

Lucas steps into my room. He pulls something from behind his back. Two blue and gold pompoms! They are made from strips of Mom's scrapbooking paper. The fringes are taped to two yellow pencils. I can tell he's worked hard on them.

"Ta-da!" Lucas cries, shaking the homemade pompoms. "Go, Muskrats!" He holds the pompoms out to me. "Now you are a *real* cheerleader!"

I take the paper pompoms from Lucas. They are not regulation size. They do not glitter. And sticky wads of tape hold them together. Still, they are the best pompoms I have ever seen. I give Lucas a big hug. Bea is right. Sometimes even annoying little brothers can be very sweet!

"Thank you," I tell him. "These pompoms will bring me good luck at tryouts. They're even better than a lucky sweatshirt!"

Lucas squirms out of my hug, but his face is beaming with pride.

I tuck the pompoms inside my backpack. Then I hurry downstairs and head out into the sunshine.

※ ※ ※

A glittery blue and gold sign greets Bea and me when we arrive at school.

In just a few hours, I'll know if I'm a Middleton Middle School cheerleader. I'll know if I'm a poppy or a *floppy*.

"Let's practice the Snap, Crackle, Hop! before the first bell," Bea suggests.

I agree and we both head to the open area by the giant muskrat statue. Dropping our backpacks on the leaf-speckled grass, we get ready to snap, crackle, hop!

But just then we hear a sound.

"Achoo!"

Bea and I look behind the muskrat. Grace and Katie are crouching there!

Grace sneezes again. "Darn these allergies," she says, taking a tissue from her pocket and blowing her nose.

"What are you two doing back there?" I ask. "Playing hide-and-seek?"

Grace and Katie exchange glances. "Um . . ." they say, coming out from behind the giant statue. "Not exactly . . ."

Bea squints, suspiciously. "Were you spying on us?"

Grace and Katie look at each other again. "Let's tell them the truth," Katie says.

Grace nods. "Yes, we've been spying for Annelise all week. She's paying us in candy to keep an eye on you. She's afraid you will do better than her at tryouts and she won't get a spot on the squad."

"That's crazy," I say. "She's a much better cheerleader than either of us."

"But everyone likes you better," Grace says. "Friendliness counts."

"We showed her your fancy jump," Katie confesses, "but we left out the clapping part."

"But that's the best part," I say. "Why would you leave it out?"

Katie shrugs. "We like you too. And we're tired of Annelise always getting her way."

A school bus pulls up to the curb. A bunch of kids get off, including Annelise. She is wearing a Muskrat cheerleading hoodie and skirt. She's carrying a pair of regulation-sized blue and gold pompoms! Her parents must have bought the whole outfit. Glittery hairspray shimmers on her ponytail, just like mine. She's also wearing glittery makeup. The hairspray and makeup definitely make her sparkle, but they don't make her shine. She may have swiped part of our routine, but thanks to Grace and Katie, she doesn't know the best part. There's still a chance I will outshine her at tryouts!

❀ ❀ ❀

Classes seem to take forever. Lots of us are on edge because of cheerleading tryouts. Even Mrs. Larson notices. She finishes her lesson early and gives us free time at the end of class to play games on the computer, read, and talk quietly until the bell rings.

When Bea and I get to the football field after school, Jenny waves us over and we get busy doing stretches and running laps. It calms us down, at least for now. "I'm beginning to think exercise is our secret weapon!" I tell Bea.

Bea nods. "We are in better shape today than we were a week ago, thanks to all our practicing! You're ready for this, Vicka. You've worked hard. You have school spirit!"

I think about what Bea said. All the running and stretching Jazmin has us doing is getting my body in good shape. But in other ways, I'm getting in better-than-average shape too. Last week, I thought being a cheerleader would make me popular. Now I know that perfect cartwheels and glittery pompoms don't make you a poppy. Only being a *real* friend can do that. I also know that if I don't make the cheerleading squad, I will be really bummed because I like exercising and yelling loudly! But even if I *flop* as a cheerleader, I can still shine as a sister and as Bea's best friend — and now as Jenny's friend too!

The judges arrive. Each one carries a clipboard with a scoring chart on it.

Jazmin sets a cooler of ice water on the team bench. "Let's go, Muskrats!" she shouts cheerfully.

"You've all worked hard. You are ready for this! I only wish we had room for everyone on the squad. But as you know, only four spots are available this year."

Bea and I squeeze hands for good luck. Then we sit on the grass and wait for our turn to perform. Jenny sits next to me. Grace and Katie start to walk over to us, but Annelise calls them over to where she is sitting on the bench. She pushes our backpacks onto the ground to make room for them.

Grace and Katie look at us. Then they sigh and walk over to Annelise.

"I thought they were done letting her boss them around," Bea says.

I shrug. "Sometimes it can take a while for stickiness to wear off."

"Jenny and Tara, you are first," Jazmin says when the judges are ready to begin.

Tara jumps up and runs onto the field, but Jenny fidgets beside me. She seems nervous today, even though she's got a great routine.

I squeeze Jenny's hand. "Good luck!" I say. "You will do great!"

Jenny smiles with relief. "Thanks, Vicka. So will you!"

Jenny joins Tara in front of the judges. They do their routine perfectly. Tara is good, but Jenny really shines! Everyone applauds for both of them when they finish. Jenny hurries back to us, smiling, as the judges mark their score sheets.

"You were awesome!" I tell her.

"Your cartwheel was great!" Bea adds.

Jenny collapses onto the grass. "Thanks!" she says, breathlessly. "I was so nervous!"

"But you are the best cheerleader here," I say with surprise. "Why would you be nervous?"

"I love doing the jumps and stuff," Jenny explains. "But other than doing silly skits, performing for others scares me. Thanks for boosting my confidence, Vicka! It really helped."

I'm glad I could help Jenny do her best. I guess

even talented people think of themselves as *unfortunately average* sometimes! And even though I don't have a lot of confidence in myself, I'm happy I could give some to Jenny.

Some of the other girls perform their routines. You can tell they practiced hard, just like Bea and me. *Everyone* wants to be on the squad!

Bea nudges me as the judges mark their score cards. "I bet we're next," she says. "My stomach is in knots!"

"My stomach is doing somersaults," I reply. "It feels like I just stepped out of a flight simulator."

Bea nods. Then she fake barfs.

I giggle. Then I fake barf too.

Jenny joins in.

"Welcome to Barfdom!" I shout.

Annelise looks over and makes a face. "Disgusting," she says, fluffing her pompoms.

Seeing her pompoms reminds me of the good luck charm Lucas gave me.

I run to my backpack and pull out the paper pompoms. They are crumpled from falling on the ground when Annelise pushed my backpack down, but they still sparkle with love!

Annelise squints as I straighten my pompoms' paper fringes. "This isn't kindergarten tryouts," she says. "Real cheerleaders use real pompoms." She fluffs her big, glittery pompoms again.

I look squarely at Annelise. "My brother made these pompoms for me. They don't glitter and they're not regulation-sized, but they were made with love, so that makes them *real*."

Annelise shakes her head and then huddles up with Grace and Katie again, talking to them as if I'm not there. But I don't care. I know I'm right. Love is the best secret weapon of all.

The judges call my name. Bea and I are next to try out!

I race onto the football field. "Ready?" Bea asks as we get into position.

I take a deep breath. "For anything," I reply confidently.

We look at the judges. "Go, Muskrats!" I shout, waving my paper pompoms.

But just as we are about to begin our routine, Annelise jumps up from the bench where she's sitting. "Wait!" she shouts. "Bea doesn't have any pompoms. She can borrow mine!"

Everyone turns and looks as Annelise hurries toward us.

I'm so surprised by Annelise's friendly gesture, I forget to be on my guard.

The closer Annelise gets, the faster she runs. Before Bea can get out of the way, Annelise stumbles. Then she falls — *splat!* — squashing Bea beneath her!

"Ouchies, my arm!" Bea screams. She cradles her wrist as Annelise rolls off her, dropping the pompoms and brushing leaves from her sweatshirt. "I barely touched you," she says. "Don't be a baby."

Bea cries out in pain. Tears spring to her eyes.

Jazmin rushes over and crouches next to Bea, checking her sister's wrist.

I glare at Annelise. "You did that on purpose!"

Annelise returns my glare. "No, I didn't!"

Grace springs to her feet, bristling like Poco does when he thinks he's a German Shepherd. "Tell the truth, Annelise. You just whispered to Katie and me that you were going to show Vicka and Bea who was boss."

"That's a lie!" Annelise says. "Tell them, Katie."

But Katie just shakes her head. "No, it's the truth. You fell on purpose."

Annelise gawks at Grace and Katie. "News flash," she says, bitterly. "You are _un_invited to my sleepover next weekend." Then she stomps off the field.

Grace lifts her shoulder. "Fine," she says. "We'll just have our own."

I want to clobber Annelise! But tears are rolling down Bea's cheeks.

I drop my paper pompoms and kneel next to her. "Are you okay?" I ask.

Bea nods, wincing as Jenny puts ice from the watercooler on Bea's wrist. "My arm just got twisted a little," she says, sniffling back tears. "Jazmin says I'll be okay. But I can't do a cartwheel today. You will have to perform our routine without me, Vicka."

"I don't care about the silly routine," I say, putting my arm around Bea's shoulders. "All I care about is *you*."

I start to help Bea stand, but she pulls away.

"I'll be fine, Vicka," she insists. "Do the Snap, Crackle, Hop! You were born to be a cheerleader!"

What Bea said isn't true. I wasn't born to be a cheerleader. I was born to be her friend. But sometimes being a friend means doing things you'd rather not do. Like Bea, trying out for cheerleading because it was important to me. Now Bea wants me to perform, even though all I want to do is take care of her.

Bea looks at me. "Please, Vicka. For me?"

I sigh. Then I pick up my paper pompoms. "Okay," I say. "I'll do the Snap, Crackle, Hop! for you. Go, Muskrats!"

Bea smiles through her tears. "Go, Vicka!"

❀ ❀ ❀

Jenny and I help Bea back to the sidelines. Grace pulls a packet of tissues from her backpack and offers one to Bea. Katie picks up the pompoms Annelise dropped and sets them by Bea's feet. I expect Annelise to march over and snatch them away. But she just sits like a lump, alone on the bleachers.

"This is all our fault," Katie says, sitting next to Bea. "If we hadn't spied on you and told Annelise you had a secret weapon, she wouldn't have gotten so jealous and none of this would have happened!"

I shoot a look at Annelise. All I want is *revenge*.

And I know exactly how to get it. If I tell the judges that Annelise is failing history, they won't let her try out because you can't be a cheerleader unless you are getting good grades — average, like me, or above average, like Bea.

The thought of tattling on Annelise is making my stomach do somersaults again. I remember what Mrs. Larson said about tattlers — they take friendship for granted. And I remember what Mom told me about getting even with a bully — it only brings you down to her level. Revenge doesn't make things better. It only makes enemies.

I look at Bea. She always puts our friendship first. It's time for me to do the same.

"Are you ready to perform your routine, Vicka?" Jazmin asks, taking her place with the other judges.

I nod and walk back onto the football field. "I would like to dedicate this cheer to my best friend, Bea. And to my brother, Lucas, who made these pompoms for me." I give my paper pompoms a shake.

"*Awww,*" the judges say. "That's so sweet!"

I expect Annelise to make a mean comment about my pompoms. But she just hunches her shoulders and ducks her head, so I begin my routine. I snap, crackle, and hop better than I ever have before!

Bea is so excited she starts clapping. Then she winces in pain and stops.

I stop too, right before I'm about to attempt a cartwheel. I don't like seeing my BFF in pain. It doesn't make me feel like cheering. All it makes me feel like doing is helping her.

I walk over to the judges. "I still can't do cartwheels very well," I tell them. "And I can't do the splits at all. But I can walk my best friend home. So that's what I'm going to do *right now*."

I give my paper pompoms to Jazmin. Then I go over to where Bea is sitting with Grace, Katie, and Jenny. I help her up and walk her home.

Chapter 13

Number One Muskrat

Later, when I'm at my house again, the doorbell rings.

Ding-dong!

When I go to the door, I'm surprised to see Jenny and Jazmin standing on my front steps.

"We think it was very nice of you, taking care of Bea when she was hurt," Jenny says. "After you left, everyone agreed that you have more team spirit than any of us. That makes you the number one Muskrat in Middleton!" Jazmin nods in agreement. Then she hands me my paper pompoms.

"But I left the competition. I can't be number one if I'm a quitter."

"You didn't quit," Jenny replies. "You gave up something for a friend. That's different."

"We all think you would shine as a cheerleader," Jazmin says to me. "But as you know, there are only four spots open on this year's cheerleading squad. In order to be fair to all the girls, we gave those spots to the four best competitors who completed their routines."

I nod in agreement. "Who did you pick?"

"Grace, Katie, Annelise, and . . . Jenny!"

Jenny smiles. "I couldn't have done it without you, Vicka. You gave me the boost of confidence I needed at the last moment."

"Congratulations!" I tell Jenny, giving her a quick hug. "You deserve to be on the squad. So do Grace and Katie." I don't say anything about Annelise. I'm sure she performed a perfect routine, but I think she failed in other ways.

"We know Annelise hurt Bea on purpose," Jazmin tells me. "Before she performed, she told us the truth about being jealous of your routine. She apologized to the judges and to Grace and Katie, for making them spy on you. She also promised to apologize to Bea. Even though what she did was wrong, we decided to give her a second chance. She's on the squad, but she's on probation. We expect her to do better."

I can't believe Annelise told the truth and apologized! If the squad can give her a second chance, maybe I can too.

"I wish you were on the squad, Vicka," Jenny says. "We all do."

I sigh. "I really *did* want to be a cheerleader, but for the wrong reasons. I thought it would make me more popular, but I'm learning that it's not what you do that makes you a poppy. It's who you are that makes you shine."

"That's the kind of team spirit the squad needs, Vicka!" Jazmin exclaims. "We'd like to offer you a special role."

I make a puzzled face. "But all the spots are taken."

Jazmin and Jenny exchange a secret smile. "There's still one left!" Jenny says. "Tell her, Jazmin, before I do!"

Jazmin hurries down my front steps and picks up a Muskrat duffel bag that's lying on the walk. She unzips it and pulls out something big, brown, and bulky. At first I can't imagine what it is, but then I see furry boots, and a grinning muskrat mask. It's the school mascot costume!

Jenny hops with excitement. "We want you to be our new Middleton Middle School mascot!" She clamps her hand over her mouth. "Oops!" she says. "I can't keep a secret!"

My mouth drops open. "Me? But what about Drew?"

Jazmin laughs. "Drew only did it once because his sister paid him. We really want you to be our number one Muskrat!"

"Please say you'll do it!" Jenny puts in. "You'll be on the squad! We need you to help us cheer the team on to victory!"

I look from Jenny to Jazmin. They are both smiling.

I look at the muskrat mask. "What about my glasses?" I ask. "Is the mask big enough to fit over them?"

"Let's find out," Jazmin says, putting the mask on over my head. It fits perfectly.

"Go, Muskrats!" I shout.

Jenny beams. "Go, Vicka!"

Chapter 14

Second Chances

After Jenny and Jazmin leave, I make a decision.

I call Annelise.

She sounds very surprised to hear my voice.

"Congratulations on making the squad," I tell her. "You will be a great cheerleader."

Annelise doesn't say anything. Maybe she thinks this is a prank call? Then I hear her take a big breath. "Thanks," she says. "I'm sorry I tried to steal your routine. It was really good, and I was jealous. I called Bea and apologized to her too."

"Thank you," I say. "And I'm sorry I called you names, even if it was only to Bea."

"What did you call me?" Annelise asks.

"Annebeast," I reply.

Annelise snorts a laugh. "My brother calls me that too."

"It looks like we'll get to do the Snap, Crackle, Hop! together, at our first football game," I say. "I'm on the squad now as the school mascot."

Annelise laughs. "You want to dress up in a silly costume and act like a goofball in front of everyone?"

I think for a moment. "I come from a family of goofballs," I reply. "Being goofy makes everyone shine. So yes, I want to dress up like a muskrat, cheer for my team, and hang out with my new friends."

Annelise is silent again. Then she asks, "So why are you calling me instead of your friends?"

"Because there's something I want to ask you. Will you be my study buddy? With cheerleading practice and games, I'm going to be extra busy so I need to get extra organized. If we study history together, it will help me a lot."

"That's crazy," Annelise says. "I'm *failing* history. You don't want my help."

"You're only failing because you haven't tried to do your best. If we both try harder, we'll both do better."

Annelise thinks this through. Then she says, "Okay. We can study together. And afterward, if you want, I can teach you how to do a cartwheel that ends with the splits."

I smile. "And I'll teach you the clap for the Snap, Crackle, Hop! It's the best part!"

When I set down the phone a minute later, I wouldn't say Annelise is one of my new *friends*. But she is my new study buddy and my new teammate. That's a hop in the right direction.

❀ ❀ ❀

Things didn't go exactly as I planned with cheer-leading. But, in the end, I think they went better than I could have imagined.

I get to be on the cheerleading squad, but I don't have to do perfect cartwheels or the splits. *Yay!*

My parents are proud of me for doing my best.

Sofia says only people who are crazy with confidence are nutty enough to jump around and cheer in front of a crowd.

Lucas thinks it's the coolest thing ever to have a sister who is the Middleton Middle School mascot. All his friends agree. One of them even asked me for my autograph! At least I'm a poppy with the kindergartners.

Bea can't wait to cheer for me from the sidelines while I cheer for our team.

Poco is back to being my pal, now that I've started taking him for walks again and stopped feeding him cornflakes.

Most of all, I know I will *shine* even when I'm covered with fur.

Not because I'm on the cheerleading squad.

I'll shine because I'm Victoria Torres . . . fortunately me!

About the Author

Julie Bowe lives in Mondovi, Wisconsin, where she writes popular books for children including *My Last Best Friend*, which won the Paterson Prize for Books for Young People and was a Barnes & Noble 2010  Summer Reading Program book. In addition to writing for kids, she loves visiting with them at schools, libraries, conferences, and book festivals throughout the year.

Always looking
for her way to shine!

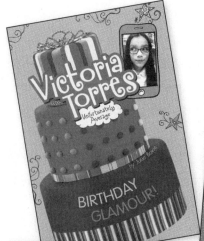

Want More Victoria Torres?

Read the first chapter of...

Face the Music

"Stop sticking Nature Nibbles up your nose, Lucas," I say to my little brother on Saturday morning. "*Ewww!* Don't eat them now! Help me find the cordless phone so I can call Bea."

Lucas ignores me as I hunt between the couch cushions in our living room. He's watching cartoons and munching on dry cereal that looks like a bowl of gravel. Our mom thinks sugary cereal is bad for us, so she only buys the kind made from oats, bran, and tree bark, I think.

I have my own phone, but it's all the way upstairs and I'm in a hurry to call my BFF. Almost every weekend we hang out together, listening to music, playing video games, doing art projects, and baking gooey chocolate chip cookies. We are excellent cookie bakers!

"Move, Vicka!" Lucas shouts as I poke around him. "You're blocking the TV, and this is my favorite show!"

I glance at the television. "Is this the one about that talking toilet plunger?"

Lucas nods excitedly. "Toilet Plunger Paul! Today he and his side-kick, Eraser Girl, are saving Dimple-town from an invasion of mutant dust bunnies! Do you want to watch with me?"

"I'd *love* to," I say in a voice that makes me sound as snarky as my sorta friend, Annelise. "But it's Saturday, otherwise known as *Bea*day. Have you seen the phone? Bea is probably wondering why I haven't called yet."

Lucas points toward the downstairs bathroom. "It's in Dad's executive office," he says.

"Thanks!" I reply, snagging a Nature Nibble from his bowl and popping it into my mouth as I dash to the bathroom. Dad calls it his *executive office* even though his real office is at the music store he and my uncle, Julio, own.

There, sitting on the sink next to a tube of Sophia's pimple medicine, is the phone. Sophia is fourteen. She keeps a phone and pimple medicine in every room of the house. Personally? I don't think the zit stick is doing her much good.

Punching the speed dial, I check myself out in the mirror while waiting for Bea to answer.

Score! No pimples.

Turning sideways I can see that my hair is really getting long, but that's the only part of me that seems to be growing. In every other way, I am still *completely* average.

"Hello?"

At last! Bea!

"Hi! It's me. What took you so long to answer?"

"I had a hair emergency. I was out of scrunchy gel, so I had to beg some off of Jazmin. She made me pay her a dollar for two squirts! Stop laughing, Vicka, you know how annoying big sisters can be. Where are you? Inside a tunnel? Your voice sounds echoey."

"I'm in the bathroom," I explain.

"The *bathroom*? TMI, Vicka. Call me when you're done!"

"I'm not *doing* anything," I explain. "I'm just standing here, looking in the mirror."

"Oh," Bea replies. "Any new developments?"

I turn sideways again and study my slender frame. "Nope," I report. "You?"

"Nothing." Bea says with a sigh.

I smile, happy my BFF and I are still evenly matched when it comes to height, weight, and shoe size.

I wander into the hallway with the phone. "What do you want to do today?" I ask Bea. "Hang out here? Go to the library? Bake cookies?"

"Can't, can't, and . . . can't," Bea replies. "Remember? I have my winter recital today."

Bea takes private piano lessons. She also plays flute with me in our school band. Bea is a super talented musician. She can even play "Jingle Bells" on her phone keypad!

"*¡Uf!*" I say. "I forgot about your recital. I'd come, but I promised Mom I'd watch Lucas this afternoon. She's scrapbooking here with her friends. What am I going to do without you?"

"Call Jenny?" Bea suggests. Jenny is my second best friend. She moved to Middleton last summer.

"Good idea," I say to Bea. "Maybe Jenny likes to bake cookies too."

"Save some for me!" Bea says before hanging up.

I call Jenny. "Sorry, Victoria," her dad says when I ask to speak with her. Jen has a gymnastics meet this weekend. She and her mom won't get back until tomorrow."

¡Ay! Jenny is a super fantastic gymnast, so I'm happy she's cart-wheeling and balancing and flying around. But I'm bummed she can't come over today.

I carry the phone into the living room and slump on the couch next to Lucas. Poco jumps onto my lap, wagging his tail and giving me doggie kisses. "Not now, Poco!" I say, laughing and pushing him down. "I'm trying to plan my day."

Poco settles onto my lap. I pet his silky fur while I try to think of other friends I could call. The list is short because I am only aver-agely popular.

I could call Katie or Grace, but they're just "school friends." We eat lunch together in the Caf and chat online sometimes, but I don't actually have their phone numbers.

Then there's Annelise. She's not one of my best friends, but I *do* have her phone number. I glance at Lucas. He's still sticking Nature Nibbles in his nose, then fake sneezing to see how far they fly.

"Look, Vicka!" Lucas shouts after an especially hard sneeze. "That one made it halfway to the TV!" Poco hops off my lap, runs to the cereal nugget that Lucas just snot-shot, and eats it.

I make a disgusted face and ask myself a very important ques-tion: *Do I, Victoria Torres, want to spend the best day of the week with a cereal sneezer?*

Answer: *No, I do not.*

I call Annelise.

"Hello, Vicka," she says on the first ring. "I know it's you because I have caller ID on my brand new phone. Daddy bought it for me yes-terday. What do you want? I'm polishing my nails, so make it quick."

Annelise is one of the bossiest girls I know. She used to be one of the meanest, too, but then she matured. "Do you want to come over? We could bake cookies."

I wait while she blows on her nails. "Why would I want to do that?" she finally asks. "They sell cookies at the European bakery downtown. That's where my mother buys all of our baked goods."

I roll my eyes even though Annelise can't see me. "But it's fun to bake them yourself. Bea and I do it almost every weekend."

"Then why are you calling me?" Annelise asks. "Are you guys fighting or something?" Annelise sounds like she's hoping my answer will be yes. She loves to stir up drama between friends.

"No, Bea and I never fight," I reply. "She's just busy today."

"So I'm your second choice, huh?" Annelise says.

"Actually, you're my *third* choice, but don't take that the wrong way. Jenny is my second-best friend. You know that. But she's busy too."

Annelise does a smirky sniff. "Don't take *this* the wrong way, Vicka, but I have more important things to do than bake cookies with you. As soon as my nails dry, I'm going to the mall. My mother is buying my holiday dresses today."

"Dresses?" I say. "How many do you need?"

"Three," Annelise replies matter-of-factly. "One for the party at my dad's house. One for the party at my mom's house. And one for the holiday concert at school."

"Why can't you wear the same dress three times?" I ask.

Annelise sniffs again. "Because that would be totally boring. Besides, my mother is paying for them. I might as well get as many as I want."

I sigh. "Whatevs, Annelise. Gotta go."

"Have fun doing nothing with nobody," she quips. Then she laughs to herself before hanging up. I take back what I said earlier about her not being mean anymore.

I ditch the phone and go looking for Mom. Maybe she has time to take me shopping for my holiday dress too, before her scrapbooking party. Our school concert is only a few weeks away. Going to the mall would make this unfortunately average day feel a little more special.

But Mom is already setting out all her holiday scrapbooking stuff on the dining room table. She and her friends must be getting an early start on making holiday cards. No way will she have time to take me shopping.

Dad bops downstairs. "Don't wait up," he tells Mom, pecking her on the cheek. "I'll be home late."

Mom kisses him back. "Say hi to Julio for me."

"Where are you going?" I ask Dad. "Can Lucas and I come too?" My sister, Sofia, is at a math club meeting, but she probably wouldn't want to hang out with us anyway. All she wants to do on weekends is study for school or stare into her boyfriend's eyes.

"Working at the store, then driving into the city," he tells me. "Uncle Julio and I have a gig tonight!"

Dad and Uncle Julio are in a band called The Jalapeños. Uncle Julio sings and plays guitar. Dad sings too and plays the drums. I can't sing, and the only instrument I know how to play is the flute, but I'm a pretty good dancer! Dad grabs me and twirls me around the room singing one of the jazzy songs his band plays.

Mom applauds at the end of our dance. "Encore!" she says as Dad and I take a bow. I get ready to do another dance.

Dad kisses me on the top of my head. "No time for an encore now,

Bonita." That's the nickname Dad gave to me when I was a baby. It means *pretty little one* in Spanish. "And I can't take you and Lucas along this time. See you tomorrow morning. What shall I make for breakfast. Pancakes?"

"*¡Si!*" I say, hugging him goodbye. "With chocolate chips, *por favor.*"

Dad smiles. "Chocolate chip pancakes it is."

Fortunately, Dad doesn't mind a little sugar for breakfast!

After Dad leaves, I sit at the table and fiddle with a pair of Mom's fancy scissors, feeling sorry for myself. I don't have a favorite cartoon to watch or a club meeting to attend or a job or even a hobby! I'm not a great gymnast or musician. And I don't have tons of money to spend at the mall.

I'm just me, Victoria Torres, unfortunately average from the inside out.

"Everyone has something special to do today, except me," I grump.

Mom looks up from sorting through a bunch of stickers. "You could make cards with us," she offers.

I sigh. I like making crafty things with Bea, but it doesn't seem as much fun with Mom and her friends. They just sit around, drinking coffee and talking about grownup stuff like the price of gasoline and where to find the best deal on pork chops and who has the most kids on the honor roll this year. As Annelise would say, *Boring.*

"Can I have some paper?" I ask, sifting through the stack of holiday designs Mom just set on the table. "Maybe I'll make some cards in my room."

"Sure!" Mom says. "Take what you want."

I grab a few sheets and head upstairs. Tossing the paper onto my desk, I crouch by my bed and reach under the mattress, pulling out the candy wrapper I keep hidden there. My crush, Drew, gave me a candy bar once. Technically, I bought it. But he handed it to me so Bea says that counts as a gift from a boy. I was planning to keep the candy bar forever until Lucas ate it. *Grrr!*

At least he didn't eat the wrapper. I close my eyes, pressing it to my nose. It still smells like milk chocolate. That's the sweetest kind of candy bar there is. Drew told me so. I felt very special that day!

Maybe I should make a card for Drew? I've never given him anything before. He doesn't even know that I like him! The only person who knows that secret is Bea.

I walk over to my desk and fold a sheet of holiday paper into a card. Then I write a message inside it.

I smile as I read the words. It's easy to feel brave about crushing on a boy when it's a secret!

To Drew
From Your Secret Admirer

I draw some *Xs* and *Os* for *kisses* and *hugs*. It's also easy to feel brave about *kissing* a boy when it's only in writing.

I tuck the card under my mattress, along with the candy wrapper.

Then I slump against my bed, wishing Bea were here. Secrets feel more sparkly when you can share them with your best friend!

Find out more about Victoria's unfortunately average life, plus get cool downloads and more at www.capstonekids.com

(Fortunately, it's all fun!)